For Aidan.

When you're old enough.

Contents:

The Motel Whore

The Painter

The Vampire

The Shoot

The Boy

This is a work of fiction.

© Paul Heatley 2017

Cover design by Ben Shanks.

The Motel Whore

Part One

The Room

The room has no name, just a number. Sixteen. Upstairs, end of the row, out the way of the rest, because this room makes music. This room gets loud. This room plays percussion, the headboard banging rhythmically against the thin back wall where there are no neighbours, cutting chunks out the plaster. Sometimes the beat takes a break, but never for long.

The bed is rarely made. The cleaners that visit the motel every other day don't come this far along. Joanie empties her own trash, when it gets too full, overflowing with knotted rubber balloons, their insides crusted with spent sex. The air stinks of bodily fluids, sweat and semen and pussy, the stench sunken deep into the walls. Between men, Joanie will open the window in the bathroom, smoke a cigarette. Hot air from outside will attempt to freshen the room, but it will fail. Joanie flicks the butt marked faintly with her lipstick into the dead dirt and brush far below, adding to the pile already there. She might wash her hands after. She might swill mouthwash. The men rarely enter the bathroom. The bathroom is hers. The bathroom is clean, though the stink on the air gets everywhere. It follows her. It is in her skin.

The bathroom shines, painfully clean. Bottles of bleach sit half-empty on the linoleum floor next to the toilet. The showerhead leaks, but it gleams. It is used often, to wash, to wash the waste of customers from between her legs or inside her mouth or from upon her chest before she moves on to the next.

Not all of them will wear a condom. She never forces the issue. Pregnancy is not a concern. Pregnancy is impossible, a womb destroyed by cheap, careless abortions. Diseases are not a concern. Diseases are cast from her mind. Life is the disease. She has the life. She can't shake the life.

The cabinet above the sink is filled with pills. They are prescription, but they are not hers. The names, patient and drug alike, have been scratched from the labels. She swallows them regardless, each one a mystery to her. Seldom do they disappoint.

The doors of the cabinet are fronted with mirror. The face looking back is not a stranger. Joanie sees her every day. Joanie helps her apply her make-up. The red lips, the rouged cheeks, the pale foundation and the shadowed eyes – blue, yellow, green, black. She brushes the teeth that are chipped and yellowing. She combs the hair that is lank and blonde. She looks into the eyes that are tired and blue. She dresses the body that is thin and grey, but this only sometimes.

This thin grey body spends days and nights unclothed, spread out on the cold bed, wrapped in shadows, only the slightest sunlight piercing through the tattered curtains drawn across the windows. The men come. They knock. They wake her. She lets them in. She lies down for them. She lets them in. They take their fill. They drop money on the drawers. When they leave, she puts the greasy notes in the safe under the bed with the rest of her payment, then she waits for the next. They wake her, drifting in and out of grey dreams. Sometimes, when they are inside, she feels as though she is still dreaming. Sometimes, when they are inside, she is wide awake. Her eyes roam the water-stained ceiling. They glide along the dirty, threadbare carpet, watch a cockroach on its back in the corner, struggling to right itself. They go to the curtains, to a crack of a hole there, to one solitary beam of sunlight shining through, blinding her, warming one thin strip of her cold flesh.

The men don't care what she does, most of them. Some insist on her participation. Some want noise.

Squeal for me baby. Their breath warm in her ear, tickling. *Let me know how much you love it.*

She groans accordingly. She will writhe for them, if that is what they want. If they ask. She will go on top. She will use her hand. She will use her mouth. She will let them enter her exit. If they want. If they ask. If they pay. She will go on her knees, like an animal, her face buried in pillows that smell of sweat. Pillows and sheets that were once white, stained a faint yellow brown, as if this has always been their colour. And she will close her eyes. And she will dream. And she will not feel a thing.

Part Two

The Pimp

Joanie dresses, leaves the room. It is morning. She feels like going out, like getting something to eat that isn't greasy fast food or an out of date tinned meal brought to her by Howie. She wraps her hands around the cold railing and takes a deep breath. It has been a long time since she was last outside, under the sun, in clean air. But she can still smell the room. From under her clothes, coming up through her collar, it leaks from her pores, it is deep in her skin.

In the car park there are three teens, little more than boys, jumping on skateboards. One of them sits on the kerb, rubs wax along its edge to make it smooth. They wear baggy jeans and loose hoodies. Two of them wear baseball caps at angles and the third wears a purple beanie. They tap each other, nod in Joanie's direction, as she makes her way by.

"Yo!" One of the cap wearers. Tallest of the three, worst-skinned, acne pock-marking his cheeks and chin. "I got a quarter – that enough to get my dick sucked?"

His friends laugh. The other kid standing, the purple beanie, says "Hey, you think you could split that quarter three ways?"

"Shit," says the sitter, "if she can break a dollar I'll treat you both."

She doesn't slow. "A quarter?"

"That's what I've got baby – what's that gonna get me?"

"For a quarter I'll bite it off. If I can find it first."

They all make a sound like *Oooooooooh!* and call after her as she walks away. She makes out the words 'bitch', 'slut', the usual insults. She hears their laughter. She keeps going. Her back is to them. They are behind her. One day they will scrape their dollars together, they will come to number sixteen. They will knock on her door.

Marge sits at the reception desk. A large woman, middle-aged and miserable. Her greying hair is scraped back into a bun. The skin of her face is loose and sagging, her jowls shake when she moves or speaks. She wears a brown dress that makes her look like some kind of puritan. Her breasts hang down to her stomach, the cheeks of her ass hang over the edges of her chair. She reads a magazine through half-moon glasses, raises her eyes as Joanie enters.

"Where's Howie?"

Marge puts down the magazine, takes off the glasses. "Out back. What are you doing?"

"I brought down the takings."

"Why?"

"I'm taking a break. I'm goin out for lunch."

"You're doing what?"

"You heard me."

"What if someone comes lookin for you?"

"They'll wait."

Marge stands, expels air like she's a rocket ship blasting off. "I'll get

Howie." She waddles through the door behind her chair, into the room where she lives with her husband, a living room with a kitchen leading off one way and a bedroom and bathroom leading off the other. Joanie leans on the counter, looks at the magazine, the article she'd been reading. The headline, running across the top of the glossy page, Sixty-Nine Ways to Please Your Man. Upside down, she reads one of the thumbnails. *Lick his asshole! Get it in there deep, and don't forget about those balls, girls! Don't be afraid to play that rusty trombone!*

The reception is plain. Wood-panelled walls, lime-green linoleum underfoot, a potted plastic plant in one corner is the only attempt at decoration. Joanie rests against the counter, looks out at the car park through the glass entrance. The three boys take turns scraping their skateboards along the waxed kerb. The purple beanie falls, scrapes his elbow. The other two gather round to watch as he picks gravel from the wound, wipes bloody fingers on his ill-fitting jeans.

A mangy cat, skinny with clumps of fur missing, writhes and stretches out on the hot tarmac. It rolls quickly onto its stomach, creeps toward the bushes. Rodents, probably. It stands, shoulders hunched, stalks its way closer.

There is little other movement around the motel. The men and women that live here, when they do leave the confines of their small rooms, they move slow, staring down at shuffling feet with hunched bodies, all will gone from their lives. They go out to buy food, they go out to buy alcohol. They come back. They knock on number sixteen. They sleep away the days and live by night.

There is a pick-up by the door, a vintage red Corvette is parked beside it, the paint scratched, the colour fading. The car is Howie's. Joanie remembers the first time it rolled into view. She'd still walked the streets then, the downtrodden side of the tracks, three towns over. Howie took her for a ride. He filled her mouth then he filled her ear.

"Come work for me," he said.

She laughed.

"I'm serious, girl. Me and my wife, we run a motel. Nice little place. We'll get you a room, get you set up. No more of this night walking bullshit, out in the freezing cold. That coat, that ain't real fur, is it? Shit, even if it was, it won't keep you warm none. When I picked you up, you were practically blue. Come with me. I'll take care of you, honey."

"Slim wouldn't like it."

"Who the fuck's Slim?"

"He's my daddy."

"Tell him you're retiring. He ain't ever gonna see you again, not out where we are. Shit, don't tell him anything at all. Just up and leave. You've never gotta come back here again, you don't wanna."

"Slim's girls don't tell him when they're done. He tells them."

"So ain't none of them have ever just up and disappeared, huh?"

"A few, but they always turn up eventually, and they're usually dead."

"Dead? He kill them?"

"No, he don't. Drugs, mostly. Don't see a girl for a few days then next thing you hearin her body's been found, dead since the last time you saw her. There was this one girl I knew, she was called Betty-Sue, they found her on a mattress in a condemned building, all curled up, rats crawlin all over, and they were eatin her. Said most of her face was gone, all chewed up."

"That how you wanna go out? Rats snackin on your face?"

"That ain't how anybody wants to go out."

"Then just disappear. Be a new kind of girl, one that ain't gonna show up dead. Come with me."

"Your wife, she's on board with it?"

"Hell, this whole thing's her idea. And darlin, believe me when I say, you ain't ever gonna get an offer as good as this one again."

The door opens, Howie steps behind the desk. Joanie turns to face him. "You brought the money down?" he says.

Joanie hands over her purse. "I need some now," she says. "I'm goin out."

Howie scratches the back of his neck. Arm raised, she can see the yellowing pit stains seeping through his white shirt. "Where you goin?"

"Out. Gonna get lunch somewhere. I'll be a coupla hours, max."

Howie is shorter than his wife, but has the same wobbling jowls. The skin on his cheeks is acne-scarred like on the three kids outside, and black and grey hair sticks out in wild tufts from the sides of his head around his ears, and the top of his head is bald and shiny with grease. He counts out the crumpled bills from her purse with hairy-knuckled fingers, thick like sausages. "What's it like up there? You stayin busy?"

She shrugs with one shoulder. "Same old, same old. Every so often someone new shows up. Sometimes they come back, sometimes they don't."

Howie nods. "One day real soon we're gonna get a girl in the room next to yours. Give a little variety, know whut I'm sayin? Give a little...*choice*. People like to have choices."

"Sure," Joanie says. Howie has always talked of more girls, for as long as she has known him.

Once we've got enough money saved, me and Marge're gonna expand this whole court, stretch it out another few rows. Get a few more girls in then, huh? Take some of the burden offa you. By that time you could be thinkin about retiring. Y'know, when that day comes, me and Marge won't forget everything you've done for us here. You've been a loyal employee, I mean that sincerely. We'll take care of you, don't you worry.

Howie looks at her for a long time, like he's trying to decide if something's different. Joanie looks at the money clasped, forgotten, in his paw. "You gonna give me that?"

"Hey, sure. What d'you think you're gonna need?"

"How about you just pay me and I'll see to myself."

He looks at her through one eye. "Where you goin?"

"For lunch."

"This ain't like you."

"It ain't. But today I feel like gettin out. Feel like eatin somethin I didn't scrape from a tin can."

"Today your birthday or somethin?"

"No."

"You're goin alone?"

"Yes."

"You sure? You ain't gonna take your little friend with you? What's his name – Rodent?"

"Rodansky."

"Same fuckin difference."

"I'm flyin solo."

"He could probably do with a walk. I swear, I go past his room and the stink that comes out is somethin else."

"It's not that bad."

"It's bad enough. And it's what it *is*. I ain't a dummy. You start doin that shit with him, then you and me're gonna fall out big style, you understand?"

"I understand this time, last time, and the time before that."

"Marge ain't happy about it. She don't like it at all. She tells me to kick im out."

"Half your guests are doin the same shit he's doin. That's why they come here. You give him the boot, you'd have to give it to all of them, too."

Howie studies her a little longer, that same look on his face like he's suspicious of something, then double checks her cut. He takes his time. He slides the money towards her. Joanie counts it.

"I'll see you when you get back," Howie says.

"Business or pleasure?"

Howie glances back over his shoulder, makes sure Marge hasn't reappeared. "Maybe both."

Joanie puts the notes in her purse, raises her eyebrows. "Maybe."

Outside, the purple beanie is still picking gravel from his arm. The other two sit with him, watching, perched on their skateboards and rolling from side to side. Joanie feels eyes. She looks to her left. Sees smoke rise from the burning tip of a cigarette. Realises a man is there, his skin so dark he is almost lost in the shadows. He leans against the frame of his open door, the room behind him pitch black. Joanie sees the whites of his eyes. He is watching her. She's seen him before, but never to talk to. Young guy, maybe pushing thirty, or just into it. Shaved head and a thick beard. Thin but not scrawny, his arms corded with gnarled muscle. Never says anything, but watches everything. He has never been to room sixteen.

He smokes his cigarette. Joanie nods at him, can't see if he returns it. She turns away, walks. Passes the three boys. None of them says anything. She passes by the pool that is rarely used, hears the hum of the barely-functioning filter. Rodansky told her once he'd seen a guy lying face down in it one night. The underwater bulbs that lit it still worked back then, though they'd flickered, flashing the image of the floating silhouette so he'd had to watch for a long time before he could be sure if the body was facedown or just lying on its back.

She'd asked, "What happened to it? Where'd it go?"

"Mr Howie came and got it. Pulled it outta the water. Put it in the trunk of his car, then he drove off. I don't know where he took it, but I don't think it was the morgue."

"He was dead?"

"Looked that way to me. He was facedown in that water a hell of a long time, I don't think there's anyone out there could hold their breath that long."

"How'd he end up in the pool? He high?"

"I don't know. That or he killed himself."

She leaves the court, makes her way to the road that runs behind the motel. All the way, until she turns the corner, hides herself behind the building, she can feel the eyes, those white eyes in the darkness, upon her back, watching her go.

She walks through town and goes into the first diner she sees. The pinewood walls are decorated with out of state license plates and caricatures of red skinned Native Americans smoking cigars. She takes a booth at the back, in the corner, where she can see the rest of the diner and out the window. Nearby are the toilets, but instead of the doors being marked MALE and FEMALE one door has a framed picture of Fred Astaire and the other has a framed picture of Ginger Rogers.

The seats in her booth, in all the booths, are red leather, cracked in places but comfortable. On the table before her someone has carved their initials – JC. She thinks of Jesus Christ. She pictures Jesus Christ sitting at the table cutting his initials into the wood, using the nails they put through his hands to pin him to the cross.

The waitress waits until she settles then takes her time coming over, a disinterested flat-footed swagger. She chews gum. Joanie has money in her pocket and she feels flush so she orders a steak. Gets fries with it, some onion rings, pepper sauce. The waitress watches her out the corner of her eye while she jots down her order. She is not courteous. "It won't be long," she says walking away, her back already turned.

Joanie thinks she has an appetite. The food comes and her appetite leaves. She picks at her plate. The onion rings are moist, the fries are cold, the steak is overdone. She puts meat in her mouth, chews it. It tastes like death, like ash.

The diner is quiet, empty save for an elderly couple that sit by the window further down, holding hands across the table. Joanie looks out the window, sips iced tea. The bartender and the waitress that served her talk at the bar. They might be flirting with each other. The waitress giggles.

Joanie takes her time. Watches the street outside, cars and people passing by. A man walks by the window, his shoulder pressed against the glass for support. He pushes a shopping cart piled high with broken televisions. His clothing is heavy and hangs around him, his hair is long and brown and he shakes it from his face, and his beard hangs all the way down to his stomach. He has objects plaited into it – beads, shells, twigs, jewellery, and an action figure. He stops before he is out of view, pauses for breath. He looks into the diner, sees Joanie watching him. He smiles, flashes pink gums that are missing teeth, and what teeth are there are black and rotten down to stumps.

When he is gone, she tries to eat a little more food. Almost gags on another piece of meat, spits it into a napkin and dumps it on the plate. She nurses her drink, not ready to go back to the motel but feeling like once she leaves she has nowhere else to go.

The waitress comes over to her table, looks at the plates, still almost as full as when she'd delivered them. "You about done here?"

Joanie holds her glass. "With the food."

The waitress is young, thin, red-headed, but she isn't pretty. She has a piggy nose and buck teeth, her eyes are too close together and she has too many freckles for anyone to think they look cute. She gathers up the plates, looks at the food barely touched, asks "Everything all right for you?"

"Everything was fine," Joanie says.

She feels like they want her to leave. She stays right where she is. She'll leave in her own time. She watches the waitress take her dishes through the back, then return to the front and continue her conversation with the bartender. The waitress isn't giggling anymore. They look in her direction a couple of times. Joanie looks back. They don't stare for long.

The old couple get up and leave. The man puts on a fishing hat with hooks and colourful flies in the rim. He smiles at the staff on his way out, tips his hat to them. The staff wave them goodbye, all smiles and happy voices. "See y'all next time." Probably regulars.

Joanie finishes her drink, leaves as a group of teenaged girls come in, most of them wearing miniskirts and knee high socks and talking on cell phones. She doesn't bother waving to the waitress and the bartender, doesn't flash them a smile or expect a cheery call to return soon.

The sun beats down hot, relentless, burns against her cold, pale skin. Joanie reaches into her bag, takes out a handful of pills, swallows them. She doesn't want to go back, not yet. She walks the other way. Passes a police car sitting stationary at the kerb, two officers inside, they watch her go by. Eyes everywhere. Eyes all upon her. *Little early in the day to be wanderin the streets, ain't it, miss?*

But no one speaks. They just watch her, teetering on heels, out of practice. She passes a guy sitting with his back to the wall of a gun store, arms resting on his knees, beard like a bird's nest, cracked sunglasses hiding his eyes, a cowboy hat pushed back on his head, the brim stained through with sweat. He wears a chequered shirt, unbuttoned to his stomach with the sleeves rolled up. There are tattoos across his knuckles, but they are faded and illegible. On the ground between his boots is a tin can and a cardboard sign with the scrawled message *IF I DINT NEED YORE FUCKIN CHARRITY I WOODNT ASK FOR IT*.

Joanie goes to the park, sits on one of the benches circling the water feature. Pennies glisten at the bottom of the pool. The feature is marble, a cherub on a cloud pouring water. Someone has sprayed a swastika on its stomach, put a glove on the end of its water bowl. A condom floats by on the water, occasionally splashed aside by the downpour. It's better than a dead body.

A woman comes along. She drags a pushchair behind her, but it holds no baby. Instead it is laden with plastic bags, the contents knock and rattle, sound like tin cans and glass bottles. She wears a heavy black coat despite the heat, has a tattered purple scarf wrapped around her neck and shoulders. Her hair is kinky and wild, grey in colour, and her head twitches to the left. She pauses by the pool, looks in, licks her lips and talks to herself. She leans over, reaches down, pulls out pennies, shovels them into her pocket. Does it again. Doesn't bother to roll up her sleeve and it is dripping wet. Three handfuls later she straightens up, satisfied, rattles her pocket to hear the coins jingle. Licks the water from her fingers. Turns her twitching head to Joanie, smiles with a mouthful of broken and misshapen teeth, drags her pushchair over.

"You ain't gonna tell on me now, is you, honey?" She drips water onto the hot ground.

"No."

The smile widens. The twitching calms. "Good girl, honey, you's a good girl. You know what I'm gonna do? I'm gonna take these pennies, and I'm gonna make these wishes come true, you hear? Every handful I grabbed, I'm gonna take them away and grant they wishes. It's somebody's lucky day, honey. You know who I is?"

"Who?"

She leans closer, conspiratorial. She smells of sweat and fire smoke, of pot and whisky and wine and gin, of burger grease and chicken fat and French fries. "I'm the wishmaster. This pool here, this pool is my duty. It's on my rounds. You ever throw a wish in there?"

"No."

"Maybe you should, honey. Maybe one day I'll pick out one a *your* wishes."

"Maybe I'll start."

"Give me your hand."

Joanie holds out her right hand.

The woman reaches into her pocket, pulls out a wet penny, places it in Joanie's palm and closes her fist around it. "You look after this one for me. Take good care of it, you hear? That there, that's someone's hopes and dreams. Ain't nobody wishin on the unimportant shit. You know what you got when you got someone's hopes and dreams? You got their *life*, honey. You got every little piece a them. So you *gots* to take good care of it, the way I take care of all a these." She jingles her pocket again. "You keep hold of it a few days, take care of it, see how it makes you feel. Trust me, honey, you'll get the energy from it the way I do. You'll *feel* everything it's got inside. Then when you got that good feelin inside a you, you come right back here and put it back in that water, where it belongs. Because that's somebody's wish, and that wish is my responsibility. You understand me, honey?"

Joanie thinks of Howie. He used to call her 'honey'.

The woman's hands, wrapped around Joanie's fist, shake. Her grip gets tighter. "Yes."

She lets go. "Bless you, honey. I knew you were a good one, I could tell by lookin. I can always tell." She leans closer still, the smell of her stronger now, she places her hands either side of Joanie's face and kisses her on the cheek. She straightens up, grabs her pushchair, points at Joanie's fist. "Take care of it for me." She starts to leave, head still turned, twitching again. "Take care of it for its owner. Bless you, honey. I'll keep a seat free for you upstairs, child, believe that."

She walks away, the pushchair behind her, still rattling and knocking, the sound gradually fading. Joanie can still smell her, can still feel the wet warmth of her kiss on her cheek. She opens her fist, looks at the coin. Its colour is dull from years spent in pockets, rubbing against others of its kind. Joanie flicks the coin, calls heads. It comes up tails. She opens her bag, takes out her purse, drops it in with the rest of her loose change.

Soon, a new woman appears, children by her side. Two boys. She sits on the bench next to Joanie's, lets the boys run into the water, to jump into it and splash each other, their clothes soaking through. Joanie looks at the woman. The woman stares at her, mousy hair tied back, red tired eyes unblinking. She looks Joanie up and down. The woman wears a grey tracksuit, dirty white pumps, sits with one leg crossed over the other and her hands folded in her lap. "I think you should leave," she says.

The boys shout at each other and laugh, splash, wrestle, each holds the other under the water and laughs harder as they thrash and struggle to breathe again. They try to grab the condom, to throw it at each other, but their splashes keep it out of reach. Their mother does not watch them. Her attention is fully on Joanie.

Joanie stands, walks the same way as the wishmaster. Goes back into town. She has to go back to the motel. She can't put it off any longer. It is time. She catches up to the wishmaster but stays behind her. Watches her park the pushchair outside a liquor store, apply the brakes then fuss over her bags, straighten them up then count them, her lips moving. She twitches. She goes inside.

Back at the motel Howie sits by the pool, face turned to the sun. He's unbuttoned his shirt down to his belly button, his hairy chest and gut hanging out. The boys with the skateboards are gone. Howie opens his eyes when she gets close, wipes sweat from his forehead and face with a mucus encrusted handkerchief. "Where you been?"

"I told you already."

"You were longer than a coupla hours."

"How often do I take time off?"

"I've seen three guys go up to your room, and that's just since I got to sittin here."

"They'll come back."

"You're sure, huh?"

"Where else they gonna go?"

"Shit, they coulda gone back to their rooms and put some hair on their knuckles. Why'd they wanna fuck you when they've already seen to themselves? You know what that means? They might as well be jerkin dollar bills straight down the can. Ain't no good to anybody down there."

"Howie, when I find the dick that sprays dollar bills, I'll marry it."

"Shit, I'd fuckin marry it."

"What you want, anyway? You out here waitin for me?"

Howie stands. "Yeah, I'm out here waitin for you. I been timin you. You're late."

"Yeah, well. Now I'm timed. Keep a log of it. You want anythin else?"

"Sure, up in your room. Let's talk."

He might as well have just said it: *Let's fuck*.

Howie leads the way.

Joanie feels eyes. She turns. The man from earlier, the one smoking in his doorway, he's left his room. He crosses the car park, carries a brown grocery bag. He stops halfway, watches her, their eyes lock. Joanie is at the foot of the stairs, one hand on the railing. He wears jeans, a brown t-shirt. His sinewy arms are marked darker in places with tattoos. Everything has frozen.

He turns away, goes to his room. Number twenty-three. Just a few up from Rodansky. She watches him go, watches him disappear through his door. Looks back to where he stood. Can see the reception. Can see Marge at the glass, watching. But she's not looking at Joanie, she's looking at her husband, at the top of the stairs, waiting outside room sixteen.

"You tryin to catch a tan or somethin?"

Joanie goes up the stairs, pulls out her key. "Why don't we make this quick, huh? From what I hear you're jumpin the queue."

"Sweetheart, they could be queuin round the block – I do what the fuck I want."

Part Three

The Junkie

Joanie sleeps. She dreams.

In her dream, the wishmaster enters her room, crawls like an animal and twitches her way to the bed then stands over her, peers down, smiles with those cracked teeth. *You still got my wish, honey? You still takin good care of my wish?*

Joanie doesn't answer.

Where's my wish, honey? What you done with my wish?

Joanie says nothing, wrapped tight in a blanket that covers her mouth.

The wishmaster twitches, harder, faster, until her whole face shakes, becomes a blur, like her head is about to explode.

Then her mouth is at her ear, her breath warm and tickling. *Keep my wishes safe, honey.*

Joanie wakes. There is knocking at her door. "Come in." Since Howie left she's had three visitors. She guesses they're the three she missed when she was out. Someone new enters the room.

"You there?" he says.

The light is off. She can see him outlined in the doorway, he looks round the room, trying to find her. "Hit the switch, darlin."

He does. The bulb is weak, isn't much of an improvement. It barely lights the corners of the room. The man blinks. He is thin, bald on top, has a moustache and wears loose fitting clothes. He scratches at the stubble on his chin and Joanie sees that he is missing the little and ring fingers of his left hand. "Are you, uh...I was told that I could, uh..."

"You're in room sixteen, darlin," she says. She opens the blanket, spreads her naked legs. "You're in the right place."

He isn't there long. After he leaves she goes to the bathroom, has a cigarette out the window. It is dark. The cold air coming in makes her shiver, but it feels good against her naked skin. She looks towards the town, off to her left, its streetlights glowing, lighting up the night like a distant fire. To her right is darkness. Down the road a way is the trailer park. She gets a lot of business from the trailer park.

A dog, or a wolf, or a coyote, she doesn't know what it is, howls. The moon is full, shines down on dead bushes and cracked earth so dry it looks like desert. It makes mountains of littered cans and newspapers, and picks out the shadows of scampering rodents.

Joanie sits on the end of the bed, puts on the snowy television and flicks through the channels with the sound turned off. She waits for another knock at the door. She half-watches a cop show where they shoot at a group of bank robbers, kill them bloodily then smoke celebratory cigarettes, fingers slick with red from their own wounds. Everyone is smiling. Everyone is happy. No one cares about the dead, or the dollar bills that plug the holes in their cooling bodies.

A commercial flashes on the screen as the show ends. White words on a black screen say FIND YOURSELF. The screen turns to a factory filled with furniture against a snowy mountain backdrop. The voiceover probably gives it context.

Joanie changes the channel. Finds a preacher. He wears a white shirt with short sleeves, thin arms wave exaggeratedly. His hair is slicked flat on top of his head. He has glasses and a beard on his chin about eight inches long, plaited. Behind him, the screen is fire. It pans over a statue of Jesus' face, eyes sad, blood dripping from his crown of thorns. Joanie turns up the volume, just a little.

"*Jesus* spoke to me, and *Jesus* said to me that the time is at hand, my people! The time is at hand, oh so close we can almost *taste* it! When fire will rain down from the heavens and smite the wicked and the deviant and the unjust, and leave the righteous unharmed! My people I tell *you, Jesus* did visit me in a dream and he told me it would be so! If you're out there and you're watching this and you are *not* one of my people, the time has come to *repent*! To *repent* before it's too late and you are *condemned* to be burned from the face of this earth! He told me, He told me, this is the *second* flood – fire instead of water, and no ark will save you now! And then *He* will come down to live amongst us, the *righteous*, and we will make for ourselves a *utopia*, we will walk unharmed through the fires and we will have *Heaven* upon this earth!"

Joanie watches him bounce up and down, throw his arms round, a ball of energy so potent it seems any moment he will burst through the screen and stand before her in the room, judging her for her sins.

Where is my wish, honey? What have you done with my wish?

She waits for a number to come on the screen, requesting donations in exchange for salvation, but none appears.

She turns the set off, goes to her window and peers out around the curtain. Sees no one coming. It is a quiet night. She opens the door, stands in the frame, naked and not caring. Looks out across the motel. Some of the rooms have lights on, but most are in darkness. In one of the lit rooms, the curtains open, she sees a man holding a newborn child to his bare chest, rocking it to sleep against him. He kisses it on the side of its sparsely haired head.

In the car park, one of the lamps flickers. The dark pool looks empty, no body floats on the scummy surface. At the reception she can see the dim light of the single lamp on the counter. Marge is probably sat there still, reading up on a further sixty-nine ways to please her man, or it is one of the nights they give the vampire a shift. Joanie doesn't know his name. He dresses all in black, has the whitest skin she's ever seen. His long hair is slicked back and he looks like a thinner, empty-cheeked and hollow-eyed Bela Lugosi. He sits at the reception desk ramrod straight, hands flat on the counter, thin lips pursed. He never seems to blink, and when he speaks he mumbles. Howie doesn't like him, calls him a "freaky motherfucker", but he is Marge's second-cousin, or third-removed nephew, or something.

He does the nights so we don't have to, so we can kick back and relax – but do I relax when he's out on the desk? Do I hell. I barely sleep. I'm always terrified he's gonna come creepin in my room, try ta take a chunk outta my neck. You know what he said when I asked him why he wanted the job? I explained to him, it was a pretty anti-social position we were offerin him, didn't leave much space for a healthy social life, just laid all the cards flat on the table y'know? Just looked at me with those freaky-deaky dead eyes a his and says 'I don't sleep'. Je-sus...

Joanie closes her door, grabs some clothes. A faded pair of black jeans with a split across the right knee, and a mustard yellow jumper that doesn't cover her stomach, slips on some boots and goes out, down the steps and across the forecourt to room twenty. She knocks hard, knows she'll have to wait. She checks her nails. There are remnants of polish round the edges, clinging to her cuticles. She can't remember the last time she painted them. She knocks again. Sniffs. There is a smell, but it isn't as bad as Howie made out. The curtains to her right twitch. She hears the catch pulled loose on the other side of the door, then it opens. Rodansky looks out at her, smiles. "You gonna just stand there, or you gonna come inside?"

Rodansky lives alone, mostly. Sometimes he has people round, a room full of them, though it is never a party. They will sit, heads nodding, spit dangling from the corners of their mouths, barely conscious. Tonight, he has only one guest. A man sleeps on the floor in the corner, lies on his side and faces the wall. Black dreadlocks sprout from his head and are spread out on the dirty carpet like snakes.

The room smells of smoke and drugs, sweat and shit and blood. "You need to start opening your windows," Joanie says. She sits down on a beanbag beside the door, her back against the wall. "Howie was complaining."

"Again?" Rodansky shrugs. "Fuck him." He falls into a computer swivel chair in front of the bathroom door. It is made of worn leather that was once shiny black but is now dulled from so many asses parked on it, and has a few slashes in its back and its arm rests. Rodansky found it in front of a house, sat with the rest of the trash waiting to be picked up with the collection the next morning. He sat himself down and rode it back to the motel, dragged himself along with his legs.

Joanie looks him over, tiny in the chair. He wears jeans that probably fit him snugly once upon a time, but he is so thin now they are baggy. He is topless, his ribcage pokes through, his torso a network of scars she's never asked him how he got. His arms are dotted with holes, some of them ooze. On top of his head is a baseball cap to hide his badly-shaved skull, though he hasn't taken the razor to his face, which sprouts a wispy, patchwork beard. "What's he gonna do, kick me out? He'll never do that. I bring him too much custom. The boys that leave me go right to your door."

"He knows that."

"Then tell him to shut his fuckin mouth." Rodansky plays with the peak of his cap, twists it from side to side, turns the cap round backwards, then all the way back round to the front. "He's just a fat bitch. Let him knock at this door, see what fuckin happens."

"Forget about it," Joanie says. "But you should still air the place out every once in a while."

He laughs. "I'll take that on board."

The television is on. It plays porn. Two naughty schoolgirls, one blonde, one brunette, give a sports car a soapy wash under the watchful gaze of their stern headmaster, his arms crossed, cane clutched in his right fist. The girls start to splash each other with the buckets of water, their white shirts get wet and see-through. The headmaster tightens his grip on the cane. The fucking will start soon.

Rodansky changed the room's regular bulb for a red one. It makes everything in the room seem darker. It hurts the eyes, but he leaves it in. A pall of smoke hangs in the air, always, further makes it difficult to see. Whenever Joanie leaves the room, if she hasn't gotten high, she has a headache. The drugs make the poor light bearable.

"What you been up to?" Rodansky says. "Same old, same old?"

"I went out. Into town."

"Oh yeah? See a movie or somethin?"

"I went for lunch."

"How was it?"

"It was good to get out. What've you been doin?"

"Same old, same old." He reaches into his pocket, pulls out a battered tin with the image of a Day of the Dead skull smoking a blunt, cannabis leaves in its empty eye sockets. He starts rolling. Through the stink of everything else, Joanie can smell the weed.

"That's potent."

Rodansky grins. "Only the best."

"You know how to treat yourself."

"Shit, if you ain't gonna treat yourself, who is?" When it's rolled he lights it up, takes a deep draw, puts his head back and closes his eyes. "Here," he says, holds out his arm without looking. "I'm gonna treat you."

Joanie takes it from him, inhales a couple of tokes before giving it back. It makes her light-headed. On the television the headmaster is fucking the blonde schoolgirl bent over his desk while caning the brunette across her bare buttocks. His strikes have drawn blood. The two girls kiss. There is a lot of tongue.

"So you've been in town today," Rodansky says. "And you're here tonight. Did you get a day off or somethin?"

"What's a day off?"

Rodansky laughs. "You had me worried ol Mr Howie was goin soft. What's he think of all this you time?"

"What's he gonna do? He keeps talkin about gettin more girls, but that's all he ever does. Talks."

"The day he brings a new one back with him you're gonna have to start behavin yourself, don't wanna get your narrow ass kicked out on the street."

"That doesn't worry me. It's nowhere I haven't been before."

"You're a survivor, girl." He inhales deeply, eyeballs popping from his head. He speaks without exhaling. "Just like me." Eventually, he blows the smoke out, a long thick plume that rises and becomes part of the toxic cloud hanging over the room. "Nothin keeps me down. And don't you worry none – I'll make sure my buddies stay loyal to you. You keep your end of the market cornered and there ain't a damn thing he can do."

Joanie stares at the red bulb. A moth flutters round it, settles on the ceiling above it, takes a few steps then stays perfectly still.

"Here." Rodansky holds out what is left of the smoke. "Finish it off."

Joanie sticks it in the corner of her mouth, takes intermittent draws. She watches the moth until it doesn't look like a living creature anymore and just another stain in the ceiling, up there with the rest of the dirty marks. When she finishes the joint she dumps the roach in the overflowing ash try in the middle of the table at the foot of Rodansky's unmade bed. She's seen him sleeping plenty of times, but she's never seen him sleep in the bed. Usually he passes out in his beaten old chair, or on the floor. His room is another that the maids tend to skip. They know which rooms are occupied on an almost permanent basis, and they know whether or not to leave them.

"Yo, Joanie." He has pulled the peak of the cap low so it covers most of his face. He peers out at her from under it, through half-closed eyes. "I don't wanna sound crude or nothin, but you think you can help me out with somethin down here?" He points at his crotch with both index fingers. "It's been a while, girl."

"Sure." She gets onto her knees before him, undoes his jeans and pulls them down to his ankles. His dick lies limp against his thigh.

"Don't use your mouth, though," he says. "I don't remember the last time I showered, it's gotta be pretty fuckin gross down there."

Joanie can smell the sweat from the space under his testicles and between his thighs and asshole. She uses her hand. Rodansky shifts in his seat a little, closes his eyes. She grips him soft but firm, gradually works him into an erection. He lets out a low groan.

"I don't even remember the last time I saw daylight," he says. "Just keep the blinds shut all the time. Don't know when it's day or night. Don't know how long it's been since I saw you last."

"You don't know much."

"No, it's true. The days just roll on by, one blending into the next, then all of a sudden a week has passed, a month, maybe a year, and you just feel like you're stuck in the middle of one long-ass day where nothin changes and it won't ever end. You know what I'm talkin about?"

Joanie spits into her hand, gets back to work. "I've got an idea."

"First time I got high, it was with my brother. I caught him doin it, him and one a his friends. They were down the side of the house, hidin behind the trash cans, suckin on a bong and gigglin at each other. When he sees I'm there he just kinda looks at me and says 'You can have a go if you don't tell mom'. I said 'What about dad?' He said 'Don't tell him, either'. So I agreed. My brother was a cool guy, I looked up to him, I wanted his approval. They showed me what to do, then laughed their asses off when I nearly coughed up a lung. They got me high and took me out with them, showed me off to the rest of their buddies, set it up so I'd walk into walls and trip over and stuff. *Hey, look at the stoned kid, he's fallin down all over the place.* But I got to hang out with my big brother, and all his friends, and that was pretty sweet. We were a lot closer after that, and he always kept me a part of stuff. Every drug I ever took, he had first. Probably he gave me my first hit of it, too."

"That's a real sweet story. Where's your brother now?"

"I don't know. No one does. He went missin. He'll be okay, though. He's a survivor too." He shifts in the chair again. "But my point is, all a that stuff, that was well over a decade ago, and it feels like it coulda just happened last week. I think about the past a lot. I ain't got much else to do, stuck in this fuckin groundhog loop. I remember bein a kid. I think about that. Toy soldiers and skateboards and watchin cartoons on a Saturday mornin, sat bored in school and wishin the day would end, feelin like you'd never make it to bein an adult."

"I don't think you ever did."

He laughs. "That's what I was aimin for. I don't wanna grow up. Shit, do *you*?"

"I ain't a kid anymore, that's for sure." Joanie's wrist begins to ache, her arm grows heavy and sore. She doesn't have to use her hand often, and when she does it never takes long. Handjobs were something people wanted when she was back walking the streets, something cheap and quick when they couldn't afford her mouth. People don't come up to room sixteen for a handjob. "I had a dollhouse when I was a kid. It's the only toy I really remember. It was my favourite. I had teddy bears and shit but they didn't mean anything. My grandfather made me this dollhouse and he died when I was like three so I never really got to know him. My grandmother raised me, and she used to talk about him a lot, showed me pictures. Said he was really handy, a great carpenter but that wasn't what he did. He sold insurance. She said he hated it, but he always felt stuck doing it. Said he was too scared to open up his own wood shop. Just dreamt about doing it until the day he died."

"Your grandmother brought you up?"

Joanie spits into her hand again. "Yeah. My mother got pregnant real young, fifteen or sixteen, the guy that did it split. My grandmother said she always had a feeling she knew who it was, but she never said his name. All she'd say was that he was an older man, and shoulda known better. Anyway, my mother had me and then she ran off too."

"You never heard from her?"

"Not so much as a birthday card. I don't know where she is. I'll never see her. I don't want to."

"What about your grandmother?"

"She followed my grandfather into the ground eventually. She took her time about it though, which I was grateful for, because I could always see that she was itching to get on after him. Went in her sleep when I was seventeen. Just been me ever since."

"No one else?"

"Like family?"

"Yeah."

"Just me."

"That sucks."

"It ain't so bad."

She tries cupping his balls, stroking them to help him along.

Rodansky sighs. "Hey, I don't think anything's gonna happen down there," he says. "Might as well just leave it be."

Joanie lets go, shakes her arm out. Rodansky's penis looks red where she's handled it.

He takes hold of the tip between his index finger and thumb, inspects it like something he's just found on the floor, making sure of what it is. "Think you gave me a friction burn," he says.

"Does it hurt?"

He pulls up his pants. "Nah, it's fine. You feelin good?"

"I'm okay."

"Wanna feel better?"

"What you thinkin?"

"I'm thinkin about floatin on clouds, girl."

Joanie runs her tongue round the inside of her mouth. "Maybe."

Rodansky stands, goes to his bed and reaches under it, pulls out a rolled up satchel. Joanie sees that when he walks he tugs at his crotch like it gives him discomfort. He returns to the chair, opens the satchel out on his lap. It holds his works. "Well you better decide quick, cos I'm almost ready to go."

"If we put it in somewhere it won't leave a mark."

"No problem."

"If Howie knows I've come to see you, he checks me over for needle marks."

"I thought you didn't care what he thought."

"I think if he found one he really would put me out."

"You scared of him?"

"No, I ain't scared of him."

"Thought you said you didn't care if he put you out?"

Joanie says nothing.

Rodansky looks up briefly, raises an eyebrow, then returns his attention to the needle and spoon and powder. "Does he know you're here?"

"I didn't tell him, but that doesn't mean he don't know. He's always watchin me."

Rodansky grunts, heats the spoon until the powder he's poured into it turns to a thick mush, begins to bubble. "Take your boots off," he says.

Joanie does.

"Lie on the bed, on your stomach. We'll do it over there."

Joanie does as he says, looks back over her shoulder to watch.

He sits at the foot of the bed, puts her right foot flat across his knee, searches her sole for a vein. He grunts when he finds one, holds her by the ankle with his left hand and with his right injects her. Joanie bites her lip. Rodansky draws out a little blood, mixes it with the heroin, then pushes the plunger all the way in. He takes the needle out, wipes away the blood. Joanie rolls onto her back, watches him go back to the chair, wrap a rubber tubing tourniquet around the top of his left arm then refill the needle. It takes him longer to find a vein of his own, but he finally does and injects himself and lies back in the chair, pulls the peak of the cap all the way down to cover his face.

Joanie lowers her head, closes her eyes. Listens to the blood rushing in her ears, feels her chest rise and fall with the steady in and out of her breath. The room spins around her, she can feel it, but it doesn't make her sick. It is a tornado, and she is in its eye, rising to the top, floating weightless, carried by wishes.

Where are my wishes?

She's lost the wishes. Lost all of them. Didn't grant a single one. Lives have ended. No hope. No life without hope.

She opens her eyes, sees her grandparents looking down at her through the clouds, clouds lit red by the glow of the bulb. She can't remember why she told Rodansky about them. Can't remember why she told him about the dollhouse.

Their faces are fading, she can't make them out. To her side stands the dark skinned man, hiding in the shadows, smoking cigarettes and watching her with bright white eyes, like a predator stalking prey through the dark. When she looks up again the clouds are gone, just a red ceiling marked by stains that begin to crawl, sprout wings and fly round the room, the fluttering of their wings incredibly loud, almost deafening.

The wishmaster crawls through the television, stands in the centre of the room and begins to dance to the music of the insect wings, moving side to side, arms raised above her head, hands making shapes. Her eyes are closed and she is smiling, showing off the gaps in her teeth. Her body is made of smoke, fading and reappearing, wispy coils cast off with each movement, falling like ash. On the television behind her men and women dressed in Ku Klux Klan robes march carrying burning crosses, walk out into the centre of a lake and drown themselves. Their crosses, extinguished, float to the surface next to their empty robes.

The insects stop flying. The wishmaster stops dancing. She stands, solid now, no more smoke, eyes still closed and mouth still smiling. Her twitch returns, her head twists violently off to the left. The twitch gets harder, grows faster, until her face is a blur.

Where are my wishes?
Where are my wishes?
Where are my wishes?
Where are my wishes?
Where are my wishes?
Where are my wishes?

Where are my wishes?

She shakes all over, falls apart. Turns to coins, a pile of them on the ground. Rats come, carry them away.

The man is in the corner still, watching from the dark, smoking his cigarette.

Part Four

The Beast

Joanie wakes on her side, facing the television. An explosion fills the screen. She sits up, smacks her lips, her mouth dry.

"Thirsty?" The man who had been sleeping on the floor is awake now. He is standing, his dreadlocks hang down over his shoulders and chest, they reach almost to his waist. There is a spider web tattoo at the corner of his right eye, it spreads out over the top of his cheek. "Do you want something to drink? A beer?" His voice is very deep.

Joanie clears her throat. "You got any soda?"

"I dunno – we got any soda?" He calls across the room to Rodansky, still in his chair but wide awake, twisting the peak of his cap from side to side.

"There might be a can in the bag there." He points to a paper bag on the edge of the dresser. The dreadlocked man rummages through, pulls something out, hands it over.

"You gonna eat this jerky?"

Rodansky frowns. "Hell no. There's jerky in there? Help yourself."

Joanie pops the tab, drinks the soda down in three long gulps. The man watches her while he chews on dried meat. When he moves, his long strands of hair sway together like a bead curtain.

"You want somethin to eat?"

"No, thank you."

"You want somethin else to drink?"

"I'm okay."

"I'm sorry to keep askin, but girl, you look like you need someone to take care of you."

"She can take care of herself," Rodansky says. "Ain't that right?"

"That's right." Joanie lowers her feet to the floor, finds her boots and pulls them on. She stands, feels herself sway. The man holds her by the elbow, steadies her. "I better get goin," she says.

"Shit, seems like you just got here," the man says.

"Hey, no problem," Rodansky says. "Thanks for comin round. It's always good to see you. Until next time."

Joanie nods, heads for the door. "Next time," she says. She has to close her eyes against the red light.

She steps outside, surprised to see darkness still, to feel the cold. She expected it to be morning, sun up, blue skies, birds singing. She turns back to the room. "Is it still tonight, or is it tomorrow?"

Rodansky laughs. "You're askin the wrong people."

She steps out into the car park, looks towards the reception. The dull glow from the lamp still shines, the neon sign out by the roadside still flickers VACANCY. Joanie takes deep breaths, feels the air cold and good in her lungs. She wonders if it is tomorrow night, if she's lost a day. Howie will be pissed. But Howie would have looked for her. Rodansky's would have been the first place he went. He would have kicked the door down, dragged her out by the hair. If he'd realised she was high, that she'd stuck a needle in herself, then he'd have dragged her all the way to the road, dumped her on her ass right under that flickering neon. She has not lost a day. It is the same night.

She looks to the end of the block, to her room. No one waiting, no queues. No one heading that way. It is that quiet time of the night, when everything gets so still and a knock upon her door is a rare thing. The time of the night when everything is so quiet it feels like the end of the world.

"Hey."

She spins, startled by the voice but not surprised to see the man there, in the dark, smoking his cigarette, the whites of his eyes burning fiercely bright. "Hello," she says.

"Come over here," he says. His voice surprises her. She expected something guttural, something rough, like an animal, but his volume is low, his tone soft. She goes to him, sees his face become clearer as she steps into the darkness beside him. He regards her silently, still smoking, looks her up and down. "Do you want a cigarette?"

"Sure."

He reaches into his pocket, pulls out a pack, shakes one loose and hands it to her. Joanie puts it between her lips, lights it from the burning end of his own. They blow smoke, look at each other through the cloud they've made.

"What is your name?" he says.

"Joanie."

He grunts.

There is a moment of silence before Joanie says "And you are?"

"I am Leo. Named for the month of my birth. My mother told me I would grow to be a lion."

"And have you?"

"No. I am a man."

Joanie turns her head, looks towards the reception again. Just the light, no one stood at the glass, watching. No Marge, no Howie, no vampire.

"You offer services," Leo says.

"You a cop?"

"I'm not a cop."

"Then why d'you talk so funny?"

He smiles. His teeth are as white as his eyes. "I talk the way I talk. There's nothing funny about it."

"Guess you ain't hearin yourself."

"You offer services," he repeats.

"From time to time. You got somethin needs serviced?"

"Perhaps. Do you want to come inside?"

"Do I *want* to? No. But if you got money, then it's up to you what I want."

"I have money."

"Enough?"

"More than."

"Then I guess I want to come inside."

They finish smoking and Joanie goes into the room. Number twenty-three. Leo follows her, closes the door, steps around her to get inside.

The lights are off, the curtains drawn closed and taped shut. The room is mostly darkness, lit by three small candles flickering in front of the television.

"Take a seat."

"Where?"

"On the floor."

Joanie sits cross-legged, her knees popping as she goes down. Leo goes round the room, lights some more candles. They are dotted haphazardly, on counters and table-tops and even the windowsill. Joanie watches him, watches the room slowly brighten around her, sees how he has decorated the walls with black paint, written messages and drawn depictions of faceless ghouls, menacing black shapes that stretch around the room, lurk from behind doorframes. Some of them hold hands, like lovers, or children.

Joanie tries to read the messages. Above the television there is a block of words, row after row, but the writing is too small to make out. Upon another wall is the proclamation I AM.

"Howie ain't gonna like what you've done to the place."

"Who is Howie?"

Joanie looks the room over again. She whistles. "If you ain't then don't take this the wrong way, but are you a serial killer?"

"No, I am not a killer."

"Cos this is what their rooms always look like. On the TV."

"I don't watch TV."

"How you gonna prove you ain't a killer?"

"By not killing you."

"Sounds like that could take a while. And it ain't exactly reassuring."

"You want reassurance? Then you have my word."

"What's so special about that?"

"It's all I have. It's all I can give. It is my greatest bond."

"You do talk funny."

"So do you."

"What's with all the candles? Your power out?"

"I prefer their light. It's not so harsh."

"It's not? Maybe you're used to it."

Leo stands still, his dark pupils framed by brilliant white locked on hers. He removes his t-shirt, folds it carefully, puts it off to one side on the back of a chair. His torso is corded with muscle, not an ounce of fat upon him. He looks like a tightly coiled snake ready to spring, to sink its fangs into its victim's throat. Tattoos are etched into his muscles and the spaces between them, their design and meaning too dark against his already dark flesh to decipher. Joanie stares for a long time, tries to make them out.

Leo closes his eyes, takes deep breaths through his nose, runs his hands back over his shaved head then curls his fingers through the hairs of his beard. He opens his eyes and paces a few steps back and forth, shakes his arms out. His movements make the candles flicker.

Joanie watches him, unable now to concentrate on his tattoos. "What are you doing? Limbering up?"

He stops, turns to her but closes his eyes, rolls his shoulders. "Preparing."

"For what?"

"It's almost time."

"To fuck?"

He smiles. "Perhaps." He clears his throat, makes a low growling sound, then makes a noise that is either a cough or a bark. Still smiling, he looks upon her. When he speaks there is a deeper, rougher edge to his voice. "Do you believe in God, Joanie?"

"I don't know."

"An agnostic?"

"Nothin so fancy. All I know is if He's up there, He ain't done much for me lately. Or ever."

He cough-barks again, shakes his head, paces, then stops. He bounces where he stands, going up and down on the balls of his feet. "Don't make me take off my face."

"What?"

"My mother had flowers in her hair. She named me for the celestial alignment at the time of my birth. She looked to the night sky, saw lions amongst the stars, decided that would be my spirit animal. That I would grow to be a lion – big, strong, fearless, a king." He closes his fists, beats the right against his chest. The low growl in the back of his throat is constant now, pauses only when he speaks. "My mother was a fool. I laughed at her notions. I am not a lion. I am no animal. I am something far greater. *I am*. I am a man. I am the Beast, the Beast all men wish they could be – I am the Beast of self." He beats his fist harder, like he is pounding a drum. "I worship no false deities. I do not look to the sky and search for meaning in dying suns. *I am* the God I worship."

"I never expected to find a God in a dive like this."

He sits before her, crosses his legs. His chest flexes, his muscles grow tight in his shoulders and arms, a twitching like there is an energy inside him trying to get out, ready to explode. Joanie remembers the preacher she saw on the television.

Up close she can see his tattoos better. Most of them are symbols she doesn't understand. There are eyes on his rotator joints, one on each side, and there are black bands of increasing thickness on each forearm, starting small at his wrists and growing bigger as they get toward the insides of his elbows. "You asked earlier if I was a killer."

"Yeah."

"Would it have made any difference to you if I had said yes?"

Joanie says nothing.

"I don't think it would. I don't think you'd have tried to run."

"Unless it involves lying on my back, I've never been much for physical exertion."

Leo smiles. He holds out his hands. "Stand up."

She takes his hands, lets him pull her to her feet. They are workman rough, she can feel the calloused pads. They stand together.

"Take off your clothes," he says.

It is a familiar command. Joanie does not bother to fold her jumper or pants. She lets them drop to the floor, kicks them to one side with a bare foot. Leo looks her naked body over, reaches out and places his right hand flat upon her chest. He feels her heart beat. He closes his eyes, speaks in a quiet voice. "Don't make me take off my face."

"I won't make you do anything you don't want to."

He smiles, eyes still closed. "But I do want to."

Leo takes a step back. He lowers his pants, steps out of them, folds them and puts them on top of his t-shirt. He is hard, his penis ramrod stiff, jutting out from a thatch of pubic hair that looks like razor wire.

"Get on your knees."

Joanie does.

Leo raises his fist, beats his chest again, a thudding, hollow sound that echoes dully through the room like a drum. He steps forward, cups Joanie's cheeks and turns her face to his. "I am the Beast," he says. "I walk my own path, as you walk yours. Tonight, our paths run parallel. Everything that is, I have willed it so. Everything that is to come, I will shape it as I see fit. Do you understand?"

"No."

He is not upset. "The strong overcome. The strong are triumphant. My face is slipping. Don't make me take it off."

He straightens, uses his hands to lower her head. Joanie knows what to do.

She takes him in her mouth, so deep she begins to choke on it. Leo growls. Joanie cups his testicles, bobs her head up and down, can feel his throbbing warmth between her cheeks. She takes her mouth off, uses her tongue and her hand. Other than the growling, he makes little other noise to indicate whether he is enjoying what she does or not. She looks up. His face is like stone, his lips pursed, hidden amongst the hairs of his beard, and his eyes are looking straight ahead, focussed on nothing.

Joanie puts him back in her mouth, goes deep, all the way to the back of her throat, catches her breath and feels her eyes begin to water. She cups his buttocks in her hands, squeezes, digs her nails in. Circles his anus with a finger, slides the tip inside. Slides it a little further, up to her middle joint.

She can sense he is getting close. His hips begin to move, his growl gets deeper. He opens his mouth and grabs her by the back of her head. "Use your hand," he says, and he pulls out. She does as she is told, her hand moves fast up and down the shaft, and it doesn't take long. He throws his head back and roars, his body so tense he shakes. His ejaculate sprays her chest. There is a lot of it. Joanie is glad not to have it in her mouth.

Leo gulps air, then looks down. Sees the mess he has made. He drops to his knees, lays Joanie down on her back without a word. He wipes his dick with his right hand, takes the semen that was left there and smears it in with the rest. With his fingertip he draws circles and triangles upon her chest and ribs and stomach, shapes that mirror the tattoos he has upon himself.

"How was it?" Joanie says.

"You don't need to talk," Leo says. He raises his hand, sits back on crossed legs, looks over his work in the flickering half-light. Minutes pass. Joanie can feel it drying upon her skin. After a while he says "You can use the shower if you want."

Joanie stands. Some of the fluid painted onto her drips to the floor. Inside the bathroom the walls and the tiles have been left unmarked. They are without words and screaming demons. The room is not as bleached-clean as she keeps her own, but it will do. She turns the shower on, leaves the water to warm. The cabinet mirror is cracked, a spider web that splits her face into a dozen pieces as she looks into it. The face looking back is not a stranger. The face that looks back is tired and pale and drawn, the eyes darker than usual, the make-up worn away.

She steps into the shower, washes herself. She does not stay there long. She can never get clean.

Leo has folded her clothes, placed them on the bed. He is dressed, waiting for her. There is money on her jumper. Too much for what she has done. She takes what is owed, puts the rest to one side.

"Take it," he says.

"That ain't what it costs."

"It's what I'm giving you."

"I didn't earn it."

"You did."

Joanie looks at him, doesn't argue. She pulls on her pants, puts the money in her pocket. As she pulls on her jumper she says "Do you work?"

"When I want to."

The jumper slips over her face, he comes back into view. "I mean, do you have a job?"

"When I need one."

She raises her eyebrows, sits down to pull on her shoes. "Reckon I'll see you again sometime?"

Leo smiles.

"Soon, maybe?"

He says nothing.

"Whatever. You need me, you know where to find me. Room sixteen. Upstairs, at the end."

"I know where it is."

"Then next time you can join the queue."

Joanie pats herself down, checks she has everything. She hadn't arrived with much. She sticks her hand in her pocket, fingers the money. That is the important thing. She nods at Leo and he nods back.

"I guess I'll see you later," she says.

She leaves.

Part Five

The Morning

Outside, the sun shines. Already it is uncomfortably hot.

Leo's door is closed behind her. She steps out from the shade, into the light, her eyes narrow against the glare. A man rides through the car park on his bicycle. He wears mouse ears and looks at her, then he is gone. Joanie looks to the reception. The lights are off there now, no need for them to be on. She expects to see Howie emerge, red-faced and shouting, demanding to know where she has been, but he does not come. Inside, through the glass, she can see the outline of a thin figure sat very still behind the desk, it can only be the vampire. She has never seen him during the day. She wonders how he gets home when the sun is out. She wonders where he lives. She knows nothing of him beyond the mocking name she has bestowed.

A car pulls in, parks. A man takes his time getting out, hops on one leg while he reaches inside to pull out a prosthetic and fits it where his left leg should be. He walks with a stick, the handle shaped like a snake's head, and it scrapes along the tarmac as he goes inside to talk to the vampire, to book a room. She wonders if she will see him later, if he will hear of her and pay her a visit, if he already knows of her.

Joanie closes her eyes, breathes. Feels the air enter her lungs, feels the world spinning beneath her feet. Behind her, in the rooms, she can see Leo in the dark, painting by candlelight, can see Rodansky passed out in his chair, another needle in his arm, can see all the faceless men whose names she does not know but for whom she lies back and opens her legs, can see them in their rooms, growing faint and withering. They wait for her. They stay for her.

She turns, sees the wishmaster at the top of the stairs, stood against the railing, head twitching impossibly fast. Just a flash of her and then she is gone, smoke rising into the air. This time, she leaves no coins.

Joanie makes her way slowly up the stairs, realising now how tired she is. But she has slept. She has slept and she has dreamed.

"But my eyes were open."

She reaches the top, drags her leaden legs further, to the door of room sixteen. She is back. She is home. She goes inside. Everything is as she left it, unchanged. That smell of sweat and semen and pussy that oozes from the walls. That smell that is a part of her, rooted deep, deep down in the pores of her skin, never to be scrubbed away. Never to be clean.

She takes off her boots, goes to the bathroom. Lights a cigarette and smokes it out the window, looks out across the scorched earth with disinterest, lets the smoke slowly coil from her lips, to float upwards and obscure her vision. She flicks the spent butt, adds it to the rest, then goes to the cabinet and takes a nameless prescription at random, shakes pills into her hand and swallows them down, chases them with water from the tap.

The bed calls. It is not much, but it is her bed. *Hers*. Almost. Howie's, really. Like the rest of the room. Like the clothes she wears. Like the life she leads. Nothing much is in her possession, nothing truly she can lay claim to.

Not her body. Not her life. Not the money she keeps safely tucked away. She does not feel like a human being. She does not feel like a person.

"Where are my wishes?" she says. She speaks to the room. It does not answer.

Joanie undresses. She does not fold the clothes. She throws them into the corner. She gets into the bed, its sheets uncharacteristically cool, usually warmed by the heat of strange men. Joanie lies back, looks to the stained ceiling until her eyes begin to close.

There is a knock upon the door. The door is not locked.

The Painter

The block is rundown and it's hard to believe that people still live in it. If it wasn't for the drug dealers outside it wouldn't look like there was any sign of life at all. The Dealer avoids looking at them as he goes inside, pretends they're not there. If they see him and know him and understand why he is there and what he is doing, they will not be happy. They will hurt him.

If it were up to him he would condemn the building, have it torn down. But there is, however, one shining ray of light inside, one redeeming quality near the top of the building. A girl. A very special girl. A girl called Sonia.

He would like to run to her, but he does not. He doesn't trust the stairs, the rickety-looking railing that is supposed to prevent people from falling over the side, and he makes sure to study the floor on each landing, to avoid the broken glass that might be there, the discarded needles and the bodies curled up against the wall, sleeping or passed out.

They're not all unconscious. Sometimes they're just pretending. They lie and they watch and they lock eyes with him as he passes as if they are paralysed, but they never call for help. They make his skin crawl. He looks back at them over his shoulder, like they might get up and follow him, like they are waiting for the right person to beat down and rob.

Sonia is an angel. She is an angel, and yet she lives in this Hell. He cannot understand why she does not leave.

He reaches her door and knocks, then waits. Her floor is quieter than the rest. No one wanders or lies here. There is not as much trash. On the wall next to her door there is an anarchy A painted on in red. The colour has dripped, run down to the floor, and it looks congealed, like a scab, like maybe it is not paint, maybe it is blood.

Sonia is expecting him. She answers the door, opens it a crack, and he smiles at her. She nods, lets him inside. He locks the door after himself. "How are you?" he says.

"I'm about to be better," she says. Her hair is tied back, but carelessly so. She wears cargo pants and a black vest. Her feet are bare and she wears no bra, he can see her nipples poke through the vest's fabric.

He reaches into his pocket, takes out her package, holds it up for her to see. She forces a smile. "Are you ready?" he says.

She nods, then goes into the bedroom without another word. He follows. There is an easel set up, a canvas already in place. She goes to the easel. Her paints are laid out, prepared, ready for his arrival. "Are you comfortable?" She turns her head a little, talks over her shoulder, but does not turn, does not look at him.

He sits in the corner. "Turn it round a little," he says. "So I can see you. I want to watch you work."

She does as he says then looks at him finally, raises an eyebrow to see if it is okay to proceed.

"Take off your clothes," he says. He licks his lips, his mouth dry. "Do it naked. I want to watch you paint it without any clothes on."

She does as he says, does not protest or question his requests. She takes off the vest first, dumps it on the bed. Her breasts are small but he can imagine them in his hands and in his mouth. Her stomach is flat and pale, and he can see every bone shift under her skin when she moves. The hair at her arm-pits is dark and thicker than his own. She takes off the cargo pants next, and if she is wearing underwear she slides it off with them. She kicks her clothes behind her, leaves them on the floor. Naked beside the easel she straightens up, looks at him. Satisfied, he nods. She takes up her paintbrush and she begins.

He watches her work. He grits his teeth and clenches his fists and can feel a drop of sweat run down the centre of his back, along the ridges of his spine. He swallows hard. He looks at her crotch. He wants to taste her, wants to bury his nose in the hair at her arm-pits and breathe it in. Getting up, he leans across the bed and reaches out to her, reaches for her smooth hip, but before even a fingertip can graze her she turns and slaps his hand with the paintbrush and tells him "No."

He takes his hand back but he remains on the bed, flat on his stomach. He bites his lip and breathes hard.

"Sit back down," she says. "Get comfortable. Don't move again."

"I want to eat you," he says.

"Sit down," she says.

He obeys, returns to the corner and sits on his hands and squirms while he watches her paint.

He has so many of her paintings already, more than he has space for. There is a spare room in his apartment and this is where he stores them. They cover the walls, and the ones that are not on the walls have been framed and they stand upright, leaning against other objects and against each other and it is almost impossible to move around inside this room, but still he does, he goes in and admires these works of art she has created for him, solely for him, he goes amongst them and trails his fingers along them and breathes in the smell of the paint and the paper and imagines she is there with him, still painting, that she spends her days painting for him and no one else.

And no one else is allowed in this room. No one else is allowed to see what she has done.

She has no money to give, and he won't take any from her.

So many people give me money. I don't need your money. I want your art.

His heart pounds uncomfortably in his chest. "Are you nearly finished?"

"Nearly," she says.

He groans, makes a high-pitched noise in the back of his throat like a kicked dog. He undoes his jeans, pulls out his cock. It is rock-hard. It points at her. Sonia looks over, but she doesn't blink, doesn't pause, she goes back to painting.

Watching her, he starts to stroke himself. He locks his fingers tightly around his dick and his hand moves faster up and down the length. He spits onto the head to better lubricate it. The sound of what he is doing fills the air but Sonia doesn't seem to notice, or care.

Climax comes with a choked cry. His shoulders sag and he catches his breath. Semen sprays across her carpet. Sonia crawls across the bed, reaches out to him with her brush, takes some of his seed from the tip of his penis, leaves a fleck of green paint behind. He tucks himself away, buttons up while she transfers what she has taken to the picture she is painting.

He watches her finish, and he feels better. He does not shift and squirm so much.

Finally, she steps back. There is paint on her hands. She puts down the brush.

"Is it done?" he says.

She nods, turns it away from him. "Don't look at it yet." She walks past him, goes to the bathroom. He hears her washing her hands. When she comes back she is clean. She goes to the easel and turns it so he can see.

It is a portrait. He is the subject, but it is not an exact likeness. His eyes are dark holes and his hair is wild and his mouth is open, a gaping abyss, a black hole, and bats are flying from it, or into it.

"It's beautiful," he says.

"It'll be dry soon." She picks up her clothes, puts them back on.

The Dealer looks down at the stain he has made on the carpet. "I've made a mess," he says.

She shakes her head. "I'll clean it up."

"I'll do it."

"Just leave it. It's fine. I'll do it myself." She wants him to leave.

He gives her the package. "The painting," he says as she takes it from him. "It's perfect. I love it."

She doesn't acknowledge his praise, doesn't look at him. She raises her eyebrows briefly then looks at what he has brought her. She puts it to one side but says nothing and he assumes she is happy with it.

"There's a little extra in there," he says.

"Okay."

"For taking off your clothes."

"I figured."

She goes to the easel, tests it with her little finger then inspects the tip. "It's dry enough," she says. She rolls it for him, hands it over.

He clasps it, pleased. He taps it against his head like he's tipping an imaginary cap. "Until next time."

"Yes."

He lets himself out and he hears her lock the door after he has gone. He makes his way down the stairs. The building does not seem so bad to him now. A warm glow envelopes him. Watching her work, watching her paint, does that to him. He smiles to himself.

Near the bottom he passes a man, a tall man with pale skin and long dark hair. The man looks at him. The Dealer avoids his eyes. They are too intense, they make his skin crawl, they make him nervous.

Then they have passed each other, and the Dealer has almost left the building, is almost free of it, but his warm glow, his good feeling, is gone.

The Vampire

1

Martin sits at the desk beside the storage closet. Joensen stands too close behind him. One warm palm squeezes his shoulder. His breath, asthmatic heavy, is hot on his neck. "What do you think?" he says. He giggles.

Martin makes his way through the block of glossy photographs in his hands. He moves the one at the front to the back, then does the same to the next, then the next. Joensen took so many pictures it feels like a flick-book. If he goes fast enough, the images look like they're moving. "It's like I'm there," Martin says. Joensen always takes too many pictures.

The woman, the subject of the photographs, is fat, folds of ghostly pale flesh envelop the straps of her bra and the elastic of her underwear. She is folding clothes, the clothes she's just taken off, she puts them to one side on top of her dresser. Martin has already watched her undress. Now he watches her finish folding her garments. Now she is unhooking her bra; now she steps out of her underwear; now she removes the band that holds her hair back. Her hair is brown, unwashed, dotted with white flakes of dandruff. Her armpits and legs are unshaved. Her face is squashed and piggy, a pair of little round spectacles perch on the end of her nose.

Joensen presses a finger to her nose. "Oink oink," he says.

The woman dresses for bed. The second last picture shows her turning off the bedroom light, then nothing. The one that follows is total darkness. A waste of a print.

The bell above the door jingles. A man enters. He doesn't look at them, goes straight to the movies, flicks through. He is thin, about five-ten, shaved head, wears a leather jacket with Old Glory painted on the back, the colours faded and flaking round the edges. His cheeks are hollow, his skin is pale and his eyes are sunken. It looks like he's just pulled himself out of his grave.

Joensen leans over Martin, his ample stomach presses against the back of the chair. He sifts through the photographs. "This one's my favourite." He pushes it into Martin's face.

Martin takes it from him, looks. The woman is naked, turning toward the bed to retrieve her nightgown. Her bulbous breasts sag, the tops scarred with stretch marks. Her nipples are at the bottom of these pale balloons and they point downward, toward her barrel thighs. Her stomach is rolls of fat, hanging so low her pubic hair is mostly hidden. Her skin is pale, marked with dead veins that stand out like tiny black worms.

"What d'you think?"

"Mm."

"That one's going on the wall."

"Lucky her."

Joensen giggles. He is not as fat as the woman in the photographs, but he is close. When he inhales he makes a snorting sound through his nose.

Every exhalation is a wheeze. Every movement seems laboured, Martin is amazed at his proclivity for photographic voyeurism and, especially, that he has never been caught.

The wall is in his apartment, next to his bed, a montage of high-resolution photographs collaged together like wallpaper, overlapping each other at the edges. They show women in various states of undress, most of them totally naked. Women that forgot to close their curtains, or draw their blinds. Martin has seen the fabled wall, once. He looked at it for a long time. Joensen left him to it, knowing it would take a while to fully appreciate his ongoing work of art. Martin looked at every picture. He did not know the women, did not recognise them, had perhaps passed them in the streets and registered their faces only fleetingly.

Sonia was there, on the wall, though the room in the picture was not familiar to him.

Some of the women were pretty, some were plain, some were ugly. Most of them were without their make-up, captured in that vulnerable moment before sleep. A select few were beautiful. These were stuck closest to the pillows at the top of Joensen's bed. A couple were from behind, women whose backs were turned, their hair tied up in buns or hanging loose after a long day, some with their heads turned to the side, faces in profile. None of the pictures were posed. None of the subjects knew they had been filmed.

In the shop, the man moves from rack to rack. Martin leaves the chair, stands behind the till. Joensen joins him. On top of the till is a small plastic toy in the exaggerated cartoon likeness of Marilyn Monroe, one leg crossed over the over, arms down by the side, enormous breasts exposed with hot red nipples, her garishly painted face winks from her bouncing bobble head. The one open eye stares at Martin. It has stared at him for a long time, since the day it arrived. Joensen ordered it online.

"Check it out," he'd said. He was excited. He always gets excited when he's got something to show, like a child with a new toy. "They stock all kinds – Betty Grable, Jean Harlow, Rita Hayworth – even got a few of the modern leading ladies. I'm gonna get a load for home, gonna stick them all round the apartment. Ain't she neat?" He glued Monroe to the top of the till, then flicked her little bobble head. Seemed like she hadn't stopped shaking since.

The man comes to the till. He sniffs hard through one nostril and swallows whatever he draws before speaking. "You got anythin where the girls are dead?" he says. "They don't gotta actually *be* dead, they can be just pretendin."

Martin reaches under the till, pulls out a handful of DVD's and a couple of magazines, spreads them on the counter. "This is all we've got right now."

"Workin on getting more, buddy," Joensen says. He flashes his biggest helpful-salesman smile.

The man looks them over, turns them round and reads the backs, studies the pictures hard, decides if the girls look dead enough for his tastes. He looks for a long time. Martin watches him. Nodding Monroe watches Martin.

"I'll take them all," the man says.

"Sure." Martin rings them up. He glances at the covers. One has a girl so pale she must have been painted white, stepping out of a coffin wearing a tattered nun's outfit, her massive breasts exposed, her pierced nipples much darker than the rest of her. She holds a giant crucifix aloft in her right hand, the bottom point a rounded penis head.

"I leave a number, you'll get in touch with me when you get some more in?"

Joensen slides him a pen and a piece of paper. "No problem, friend."

"You want a bag for these?" Martin says.

"Naw." He slides the paper back. He's written his number but no name. "I'll just carry em. Better for the environment, right, if we cut down on the bags. All that plastic. It's toxic, man."

"That's what I hear."

The man leaves, his films and literature piled up and carried in both hands.

Joensen rounds the counter, straightens up the racks where the man thumbed through. The store neatened, he stands in the centre of the floor with his hands on his hips, looks round. He owns the store. He is Martin's boss.

The shop is located off the main street, down a narrow alley often populated with drunks and bums. It reeks of their piss. The windows, which are blacked out from the inside with posters of well-known and unknown porn stars (*Hey*, Joensen said, *who gives a fuck who they are when they're naked?*), are covered in rusted metal grates. The sign above the door reads 'THE BACK ALLEY VALLEY', black writing on a hot-pink background outlined with tiny LED's, most of which have been smashed by weather, and birds, and kids.

The inside is not well lit, a couple of dim bulbs here and there as if to give customers the impression they are browsing in complete privacy. The front room, where the till is kept, is mainly racks. Racks of DVD's, racks of magazines, racks of dirty books that rarely sell as the shop's clientele prefer a visual aid to one imagined through words. They have posters on the walls as well as the windows, and next to the till are sold postcards with naked men and women on them. The postcards are a surprisingly high-seller.

They keep their more specialised products under the till and in the storage closet behind, the kind of stuff that might be considered extreme, the kind of stuff that might have animals in it, or women pretending to be dead.

An open doorway obscured by a bead curtain leads through to the next room, filled with sex toys and costumes and masks. There are cameras in all four corners of this room so Martin, or whomever is on the till, can ably monitor any browsing customers.

Joensen's newest set of pictures sits on the counter. His favourite image is on top. "What do you do with the rest of these?" Martin says. He runs the tip of one finger down the side of the considerable pile.

Joensen looks back over his shoulder. "I store them," he says. "For posterity." He comes back round the counter, gathers up his pictures, then goes to his desk, his computer. "Are you working tonight?"

"Not tonight."

Joensen sits in his chair, turns it to face Martin. "Could tonight be the night?" He grins.

Martin doesn't understand. "For what?"

"Come with me. Snap some pictures."

This is a regular invite, one Martin has no intention of taking up. "I'm busy."

"Oh." Joensen's smile slips.

"I'm going to see Sonia."

"Oh. How is she?"

"She's fine."

"Some other time, then." He scratches between the fleshy folds at the back of his neck. "But one day you'll come with me."

"Is that a question?"

Joensen winks. "Who knows – you might even enjoy yourself."

"Sure."

Joensen nods, then turns to his computer screen. Its sickly light gives his pale face a greenish hue, emphasises the darkness under his eyes, the acne scars on his cheeks, and the short hairs growing on his neck and top lip from not shaving. His thick fingers glide over the keyboard, tap at the letters with alarming speed.

Martin has a magazine tucked down the side of the till. He'd been looking at it when Joensen arrived, eager to show off his freshest batch of photographs. He takes it back out now, flicks idly through it, glances at the pictures without really seeing them. Goth girls, punk girls, rave girls – all naked, the only thing to differentiate one genre from another the style of their hair and make-up, and the accessories they wear round their wrists and necks and ankles. They look back up at him from glossy pages with bored or aggressive or attempted-sexy eyes. Martin closes the magazine. Monroe nods her head. Smiles at him. Winks.

"I'm going out," he says.

"Sure. How long?"

"I'll be an hour, maybe. You want anything?"

"Coffee," Joensen says. He doesn't look up. "Black'll do. And a candy bar. Something sweet. I don't care what. Surprise me."

2

Men pass through the car park of the motel, men without rooms and with no intention of checking in. They go to see the whore in room sixteen, or the drug dealer in room twenty. Shuffling, stumbling, over cracked tarmac and under flickering streetlamps, they look like something out of a horror movie. Martin watches them pass. It is almost two in the morning, the night populated with the people that hide themselves away during the day, like insects cowering from light, scuttling out from their holes now that darkness has finally fallen.

It is rare that anyone ever comes to check into the motel in the middle of the night, or the early hours of the morning. Mostly his shift consists of watching the living dead stumble to and from their unofficial appointments. Martin has a magazine. He brought it from the shop. All of his magazines come from the shop. He doesn't read anything else.

For a while he skims the articles and the pictures, hunched over the desk with the lamp on, the only sound the ticking of the clock hanging on the wall behind him. An article about a woman that writes letters to serial killers on Death Row catches his eye. She sends them naked pictures of herself along with pages and pages of handwritten sexual fantasies where she imagines she ties them up and fucks them while glossy portrait photographs of their victims watch them from the walls.

Why do you do it?

It gets me off.

Do you think they enjoy it?

I imagine it's one of the only things they get to enjoy while they sit in their cells, counting down the days.

Do they ever respond?

All the time.

Around the article and the interview are some of the nude pictures she has sent. She isn't an attractive woman. She poses on a zebra-print rug, her body soft and flabby, her thighs mottled with cellulite. Her breasts hang down past the rolls of her stomach, the nipples round like pancakes. Her jaw line is gone, her chin disappears into the fat of her neck, her bright red lips pout like a fish and her dark hair is kinky and wild.

Martin lingers over her pictures. She looks like something Joensen would put on his wall at the foot of the bed, the place where he rarely looks. The forgotten corner.

The door opens. Martin raises his eyes. A man enters. He is tall, wears a sweat-stained vest that barely covers his bulging stomach and exposes his hairy arms and shoulders despite the night's chill. A smell comes off him of cigarettes and scotch and sweat, strong enough to fill the room.

"You got change for a buck, man?" He holds up a crumpled note.

"Why?"

"I gotta use the payphone." He jerks his thumb back at the door, indicating the two payphones just outside. "I gotta get a ride, man."

Martin takes the note, hands back the change.

The man hesitates by the door. "Say, you ain't seen my car, have you?"

"I don't know."

"Whut?"

"What do you drive?"

"It's green. Lime green. Looks like somethin you wanna put in your mouth and suck on, cos you know it's gonna be sweet." The man smiles proudly, shows off a mouthful of cracked yellow teeth browning at the gums. "And brother, she's a sweet ride."

"I haven't see it."

"I mighta parked it over the road. I can't remember."

"Where've you been?"

The man laughs, scratches at his cheek through a thick beard. "Shit man, I knew that I'd be able to find the damn thing myself. You see her, you give me a call, huh?"

"Sure."

The man makes a gun of his right hand, points it at Martin, winks. "You're all right." He leaves, goes to the phone to make his call.

Under the desk, where Martin sits, there is a baseball bat. He's never had to use it. Howie claims to have used it a couple of times, says it almost as a boast. *You look close enough, you can still see the blood. Jeez, I gave it to those fuckers hard! Ain't the first time I've had to bust skulls, believe me.*

The smell of the man lingers in the air. Martin can hear his voice outside, muffled through the glass and he can't understand anything said. He looks out across the courtyard, up to the balcony, sees a few men there, smoking, the tips of their cigarettes burning momentarily brighter as they inhale. None of the men speak to each other. They smoke, flick the butts, go back inside. No greetings, no small talk, no farewells.

Martin returns to his magazine. To his left, on the counter, there is a small television. It is old, the reception isn't good. Like everything else Howie buys it is cheap. Martin doesn't watch it often. Turns it on only when he forgets to bring reading material.

He leaves the Death Row fantasist behind, reads about Japanese tentacle porn. This too has pictures.

The door opens. The man returns.

"My buddy's gonna come pick me up," he says. "He ain't gonna be long."

Martin nods.

"I took a look round the car park there, see if I could spot my ride, but she ain't here. You got security cameras out there?"

"No."

"You ain't? Maybe you should get some."

"We'll look into it."

The lingering smell has gotten stronger.

"If my baby's gone, if I can't find her, that means someone's done come along and taken her. If they done that, I'm gonna find em, you know what I mean?"

"It's not right to take what doesn't belong to you."

"*Exactly*, man! You fuckin get it!" He points the gun hand again. "Shit son, you're all right."

"Thank you."

"You got a ride?"

"I don't drive."

"How you get round?"

"I walk. Or I take the bus."

The man snorts. "That ain't no way to travel, son! You gotta have a motor of your own – that's *freedom*, man! You ain't got a car, you ain't got *shit*! You're trapped! You need the escape of four wheels, leather interior, a steering wheel in your hands and an engine throbbin in front a you! That's *power* – man-made, animal-like power right at your fingertips."

Martin blinks.

"You get that though, you understand, I can see it in your eyes. You get everythin, you know exactly what I'm talkin about. Shit, tomorrow mornin, you're gonna go out and get yourself the sweetest ride, I can sense it." The man grabs the bottom of his vest, pulls it up to his face and reveals his belly underneath, thick curls of black hair sprout from it, thicker than the hair on top of his head. There is a scar up the middle of his stomach, it runs down from his belly button, disappears into the waistband of his pants. The scar is pink and shiny and no hair grows there. He blows his nose into the cotton.

"You hella pale, son. You ain't gettin enough sunlight, I reckon. Now don't get me wrong, I ain't no doctor, but that ain't gonna be good for you. We needs the sun, son." He laughs at himself. "You look like a damn ghost."

"Maybe I am."

"Huh?"

"Maybe I'm a ghost. Maybe I'm not here, not really. There's no one in this room, you're all alone. You're talking to an empty chair."

"Shit, son." The man shakes his head. "How d'you know *I* ain't a ghost?"

"Because I can smell you."

The man roars laughter. He makes the gun hand again. "Man, I could talk to you all night! You think ghosts maybe do smell?"

"No."

"It'd suck to be dead. Man, I could be lookin for my car every damn night and not even know about it, stuck in this Goddamn endless loop, and I wouldn't even know. You see my car, you'll let me know, right?"

"Yes."

"You gotta, man. Findin that car could be my only way into paradise. I don't wanna wander forever."

"There is no forever."

The man opens his mouth, pauses. Passing lights illuminate the room, a car pulls up outside. The man turns. "That's my buddy," he says. "I'm gonna get goin. I'll catch you later, y'hear? Stay safe." He points his gun a final time then leaves, climbs into the car. It pulls away. In the dark it is difficult to make out what colour it is. It might be lime green.

Martin stands, goes to the door, steps outside. He leaves the door open to clear the room of the stink. The night is cold but he doesn't mind. He looks over the motel. Not all of the streetlamps work, and most of the ones that do flicker. There are men outside, different men from before, smoking at the balcony. On the ground floor they lean against the walls, hidden in the shadows, the burning tips of their cigarettes the only signs that they are there. Someone leaves room sixteen, goes to a car and drives away. Someone else gets out of a different car, goes up the steps to room sixteen. They are never in there for long.

Music plays from a room, too loud. Words spit-rapped over an aggressive drum beat. A lizard hops over the cracked pavement at Martin's feet. He watches it go, watches it disappear into the darkness, then he goes back inside, closes the door.

3

The outside of Sonia's building is not welcoming. Graffiti marks the walls of the entrance where today only one derelict sits curled into himself. Sleeping or awake, breathing or not, it is impossible to tell. His face is hidden in the furry folds of his hood, his body entombed within his oversized and well-worn coat.

Most of the windows on the lower levels have been smashed, likely by kids throwing stones, and where people inside could be bothered they have covered these holes with cardboard or chipboard or bin liners. The gap of one missing window has been filled with a Greek flag.

At the side of the building hang the drug dealers, passing the days in small groups that change every couple of hours. They have a steady stream of customers, most of whom come from inside the building, though cars will occasionally pull up and transactions occur through open windows. The dumpsters here are overflowing. The trash is irregularly taken, the collectors kept away by a fear of the people congregating nearby. At the front, broken glass and syringes pop and crunch underfoot as Martin makes his way inside.

Inside is not much better.

The graffiti is not limited to the outer walls. It marks the interior too, the corridors, most of which stink of piss, and sometimes shit. Bodies lie huddled in dark corners, some with belts synched tight around their biceps, needles still hanging from the pierced skin at the insides of their elbows. Martin has seen dead animals in these corridors, rats and cats and birds, one bird had been nailed to the wall, its wings spread like it was mid-flight, and once he'd even seen a dog, hung by its lead from the railing above the first set of stairs.

The elevator is out of order, and it will never be repaired. He takes the stairs. No dead dogs swing today. A man goes down, passes him, scratches at his head which has been shaved in patches. He mutters to himself. Sometimes Martin recognises the men and women he passes in the corridors. Always the same people, going up and down, lost, confused, on their way to nowhere, and even when it's not them they all look the same anyway, beaten down and broken by the world.

On the first floor there is a door slightly ajar, from inside he can hear crying. He doesn't know if it is a man, a woman, or a child. On the stairs next to this open door sits a man, his hands on his knees, a dreamy look on his face. His top row of teeth scrape his bottom lip. He smiles at Martin. Martin has not seen him before.

Sonia lives on the ninth floor, the top floor, where things are a little quieter.

Her fringe is cut short but her hair is long at the sides and back where she's tied feathers into it like a Native American. She wears a grey vest with no bra. It is loose and hangs low on her chest, and if she twists a certain way it exposes a little pink rosebud nipple. The bottom of the vest is tucked into denim shorts that started life as a pair of jeans she hacked at until now they barely cover her ass. Her legs and feet are bare. Her skin is pale, and there are bruises on her shins.

"Hey," she says. She wears the sleepy happy smile that means the warm glow of drugs earlier taken is still coursing through her. It is the same smile of the man on the stairs outside the crying room. "I was wonderin when you'd get here."

Martin steps inside. "I'm here now."

"How was work?"

"Which job?"

"The motel."

"No change."

"How about the shop."

"No change."

"Well, if ever there is a change, you be sure and let me know."

Martin sits on the sofa. The room stinks of pot. There is an ashtray in the middle of the floor filled with crushed butts. Sonia crosses the room, opens a window. It is as close as she has gotten to being outside in a while. She doesn't like to call what she has agoraphobia, because that's not right. She doesn't like to call it anxiety either, but that's the closest word she has.

They are in her front room. It is sparse. A beat-up old sofa Martin helped her haul up from the street after someone left it out by the kerb for a trash day that was a long time coming sits in the centre of the room. There are a couple of bean bags over by the wall under the window, and a portable stereo on the floor with a few CD cases scattered round it, all for bands he's never heard of. Before the sofa there was only the bean bags, and a few scattered cushions. There is no television and the walls are bare, no framed pictures of family or relatives, nothing decorative. The bedroom is much the same in terms of sentiment, though in there Sonia keeps an easel upon which she does water paints she gives to her dealer in exchange for drugs. Her dealer is not part of the group outside the building. Her dealer visits her direct. He avoids the group outside. He is not affiliated with them.

Sonia doesn't paint when he is not around. The artist's passion left her a long time ago. She paints only for her dealer, only when she wants to get high. He likes to watch her do it, create for him a work of art out of nothing more than blank canvas. Martin has never met her dealer.

"What've you been doing?" Martin says.

She shrugs. "Nothin. Were you working last night?"

"Yeah."

"What time did you finish?"

"Eight."

She checks the time elaborately, raises her eyebrows as high as they will go. "Oh boy," she says. She puts in an okie accent. "That was barely two hours ago, you must be pretty darn tired – you wanna take a nap or somethin?"

"I'm okay."

She tilts her head to the side, her gestures over-dramatised, childish and clown-like, vaudeville. She is playing a part. She waves her arms expansively and puts her hands on her hips. "Well gee, you want somethin to eat?"

"I'm fine."

She laughs. She drops the accent. "Surprise surprise." It is an inside joke between them, Martin's lack of sleep and appetite. She already knows the answer to her questions.

No wonder you're so pale.

Why don't you come over here and we'll compare tans.

She goes into the kitchen and pours herself a glass of milk, then sits cross-legged on the floor in front of him to drink it. Her vest hangs low and he can see the top of an areola. "You wanna get high?"

"Not today."

She gives him a sideways glance, bites her lip coquettishly. "Then why'd you come here? Just to see little ol' me?"

"That's it. I was just passin by. Thought I'd drop in."

"That all?" She lets her shoulders drop, still playing. "What a disappointment." She drains her milk in one go, long gulps he can see going down her slender neck. She puts the glass next to the ash tray. "I think someone's been trying to get in." She's not playing anymore, though she states this so offhand it catches Martin by surprise.

"What?"

"Into the apartment. Maybe it's more than one person, I dunno. You know what they're like out there – it's Night of the Living fucking Dead. Probably just goin to the wrong door. But a few times now someone's tried to open it."

"When?"

"Day, night, anytime."

"What do you do?"

"Nothin."

Martin looks back, checks the door like he expects someone to be working at the handle. "It's locked all the time, right?"

"Yeah. When I remember."

"It ain't funny. Try to remember harder."

"You worried about me, Marty?"

He ignores her. "Come sit with me."

She sits beside him on the sofa, presses herself against his arm, rests her head upon his shoulder. She looks toward the window, at the sky. There are no curtains, no blinds. Martin looks at the wall. He thinks about work. About the store and the motel. Thinks about the men that line up along the balcony to fuck the whore in room sixteen, and the men that come into the shop. Hooded, lonely figures, all of them. When they leave they never look any happier than when they went in. Temporary, fleeting relief from their lives, whether it is in the physical presence of a woman, or with the likeness of one, a visual aid they can clutch and defile as they defile themselves.

Sonia puts her hand on his thigh, strokes the inside of his leg.

The wall is cracked, stained, marked by the hands of the dozen or so occupants that have lived here before Sonia arrived. The paint is old, faded, looks dirty, impossible to tell when it was last freshened, doubtful it ever will be again. The building is falling apart, crumbling around all those who call it home, the junkies and hustlers and whores, the lost and the damned. The building has infected them with its decay, or else they have infected it.

Sonia presses her lips to his neck, kisses him. Her mouth is warm, wet. She sinks her teeth into his earlobe. Her hand moves to his crotch, rubs.

"Do you think you'll ever leave this place?" he says.

She speaks in a breathy whisper. "And go where?"

"You could come with me."

She laughs. "I'm sure you'd love that. You like being alone too much, Martin. You like solitude and isolation, you like it as much as I do. You're never lonely."

"I could tolerate you."

"I don't want *tolerance*."

"Well, maybe you'll leave when this building collapses under the weight of its own decadence."

She giggles. "Nope, I'll still be here. I'll take shelter in the rubble."

Martin takes a fistful of the hair at the back of her head, kisses her hard. "Take off your clothes," he says.

She stands to undress herself and he does the same. Naked, they press against each other, mouths locked. Their bodies are similar. Both pale, both thin, more points than curves. Some days, when she has not eaten for a while, Sonia looks withered, like the slightest gust of wind could break her bones. Today she does not look withered, though still the skin clings to her bones, and her breasts, as flat as they are, have the look of deflated balloons. Every rib can be counted, so prominent they have shadows in the spaces between.

The hair on her body is thin, barely noticeable save for the tufts, slightly darker, at her armpits, and the thatch at her crotch, framed by her protruding hips. She puts her hands upon Martin's shoulders, runs her fingers lightly up and down his arms. "You need to eat more," she says. It is a joke. Another one. Locked together they are so similar it is hard to tell where the man ends and the woman begins.

She puts her hands through his long hair, trails them down across his chest and stomach, cups his testicles in one and grips the shaft in the other. She kisses him on the mouth, slips her tongue over his.

"You taste like cigarettes," she says. "And coffee, cream but no sugar."

"You taste like pot," he says.

She sits him back down, then kisses his chest, his stomach, goes to her knees between his legs and kisses the tip of his penis, then slides it between her cheeks. Martin closes his eyes, puts one hand on the back of her bobbing head, strokes a feather between his thumb and index finger.

After a while she pulls away. "How does that feel?"

"It feels like the closest I'll get to Heaven."

"Not quite." She grins. "That was just the escalator going up." She climbs on top, spreads her legs, grips the base of his cock and eases him inside. She grips him tight. Her eyes are closed, her mouth is open, she begins to thrust, her bony hips rock back and forth. Martin holds her, her waist so narrow his hands almost meet in the middle. He reaches down, squeezes her buttocks.

"Turn round," he says.

Sonia stands, turns, lowers herself back into place, her hands upon his legs. She bounces up and down in his lap, breathing hard. Choked cries escape her pale lips. Martin wets his index finger, eases it into her anus. Sonia gasps. He works it up to the middle joint. Sonia takes her right hand from his thigh, uses it to rub her clitoris. From behind he can see her arm working vigorously.

He slides the finger in and out, a little deeper each time, until it is in to the knuckle. He pulls it out then holds her hips, lifts her off him until her anus is hovering above the tip of his dick. She holds his legs again, her fingers digging in tight.

"Go slow," she says.

Slick with the juices of her vagina, he slips inside, inch by inch. Sonia wriggles on. She groans. He aids her down until she is flat against him. After a moment, she raises and lowers herself slowly, finding her new rhythm, gradually easing in to it. Her hand goes back to her clitoris.

Martin closes his eyes, tight and warm and safe inside her, there is no outside world, no other people, just the two of them, a universe in and of themselves. Nothing else matters. He comes, his body shudders involuntarily, goes limp. He groans. Sonia begins to slow, though continues to work herself. She is getting close, the cries that leave her no longer escaping but released; sing-song, rapturous cries of delight. She pants, trembles. The feather in her hair shakes as if about to take flight.

 Behind them, someone tries to open the door.

4

A man in a white bunny costume hands balloons to children. The costume is tattered, greying, one ear flops broken, the wire inside supposed to hold it up has snapped. The kids are in fancy dress and they wear paper crowns, like the kind won in Christmas crackers. Behind them, watching, waiting to be noticed, stands a hot dog vendor. He is tall, skeletal thin, wears a vest stained with brine, his bare shoulders white like clean bed sheets, the thin hair on his head scraped back into a greasy ponytail.

The children are dressed like superheroes. It might be a birthday party. Martin passes by. He is in the park. Earlier, before he left his apartment, the sun was shining but now it is gone, hidden behind a low blanket of dirty white clouds that cover the sky. He finds an empty bench and takes a seat, runs his hands down his face, back through his hair, then puts them in his jacket pockets and sits back. The bench has been decorated with permanent marker, and gouged with jagged objects. Martin sees a Jewish star, a swastika, a cross, and something that might be a gang symbol. He sees names and initials scrawled inside crude hearts. Inside some of these hearts the names have been blacked out, a romance that has run its course, the evidence needing to be destroyed.

The superhero children run past him, chase each other, pretend to be flying. Some of them carry hot dogs, ketchup and mustard smeared round their mouths. They all have balloons, different colours, the strings tied round their wrists or knotted to their clothes.

The park's grass is dying, the railings that mark its perimeter are rusted and clogged with discarded newspapers and fast food containers. The ground is littered with the plastic rings from six-packs, and in the gutters lie crusted condoms. People ignore the filth, pretend it isn't there, all this evidence of what goes on after dark. They allow their children to play here, to pretend the area is a beauty spot to be enjoyed by all the town. Martin sees what they refuse to see. Stares at it for a long time, until it is all he can see, and the park becomes a sewer, a dump, a cesspit, they are sat in and swimming through filth.

A woman passes. She pushes a stroller, the child inside silent. Martin watches her go. She wears a skirt too short for the weather. Her legs are bare and from behind he can see the stretch marks round her thighs and the backs of her knees, and the varicose veins that bulge from her calves.

A voice speaks beside him, muffled. "I reckon she'da been pretty once."

It is the bunny. He stands next to the bench. Up close, his suit smells of cigarettes and the faint undercurrent of piss. In his left hand he holds the balloons he has not blown. The bunny looks at Martin with glass eyes and a hollow smile. He nods his head at the bench. "Mind if I take a seat?"

"No."

The bunny takes off his head, holds it under his arm as he sits down groaning, puts the head on the ground between his feet. The man's face is narrow, his gaunt cheeks thickly stubbled, the skin under his eyes is dark and tired. His thin hair is pressed flat to his scalp with sweat from the heat inside the bunny head. He reveals a joint. Martin didn't see where he pulled it from. "Want some?"

"No."

The bunny lights it, begins to smoke. "She's old now, the woman with the kid. All the women that come here, with their kids, they're all old, no matter their age. I recognise some of them, from back in school. None of them recognise me. I don't know you. Were you like me? Were you a ghost?"

"Probably."

"Do you know how I mean?"

"No."

"Were you one of those kids no one noticed. You were always there, but no one ever saw you."

"I didn't go to your school. I'm not from round here."

"Then what the fuck are you doing here, man?"

"I have family here. They offered me a job."

"Shit, I hope it's a good one."

"It's not."

The bunny laughs.

Martin looks at the suit. "Do you enjoy what you do?"

The bunny smirks. "I'm still a ghost. These days I just wear a sheet. Now they can see me."

"Why's it so important to be seen?"

He lets smoke fall from his lips. It catches on the wind and carries up Martin's nose. "I've been anonymous for a long time."

"You're still anonymous. You're just a man in a suit."

The bunny laughs. "Be all you can be, right?" He smokes in silence for a bit. "Do you have a home?"

"I have a place."

"I live here."

Martin says nothing.

"Not, like, *really*. I don't mean I sleep here, not all the time. But this park is home to me. I see what happens here. I see everything that happens." He takes a long draw, holds it down and shakes his head slowly before he exhales. "I don't like a lot of what I see."

"You don't have to like everything you see. You don't even need to acknowledge it."

"You don't do that, how you gonna change anything?"

"I'm not trying to."

The bunny blows air. "One day I'm gonna do somethin."

"Good for you."

The bunny stares into the distance, eyes unfocussed. "One day I'm gonna clean this park up, and it's gonna be a nice place again, a place you can bring your kids and not worry they're gonna get pricked on some junkie's needle. You got kids?"

"No."

"Good. Me neither. I wouldn't. Not yet. Not when everythin's like this, all fucked up. We gotta fix things first, that's what I'm tryin to say. Gotta make things right for the future. When I was a kid, my mother used to bring me here all the time. It was my favourite place in the whole world. There were always kids playin, men with long hair playin guitars, clowns and mimes and jugglers and vendors, hot dogs and candy floss. It was like goin to the carnival, but it didn't stink of animal shit. Everyone was smilin. Everyone was happy."

"That's how you remember it."

"That's how it *was*."

"We get older, we start to deteriorate, and the world rots with us."

The bunny raises an eyebrow. "Huh?"

"Nothing."

"Y'know, there's one thing in this park that still gets a lot a visits. The water feature. You know why? People are throwin their coins into it, makin wishes. That says to me that there's *hope*. Some people have got hope that things can get better."

"How's that?"

"They're makin wishes, they're makin a *lot* of wishes. They *want* things to be better. When I make a start, they're gonna join me. We're gonna clean this park, make it perfect. Then what's to stop us? We'll clean up this whole damn town. Make it how it should be, make it right again. How it used to be, how I remember it."

"When you gonna make your start?"

"When the time's right."

"How'll you know?"

"I'll know. You'll know, too. Everyone's gonna know." The bunny finishes what he is smoking, flicks the butt of it into the weeds, picks up his head and stands. "I'll see you again," he says. He puts the head on. "One day you'll come back here and your eyes are gonna hurt it's gonna be so fuckin radiant." He pulls his rabbit head back on. "Look for me upon my throne, I'll be the king of the park. Come find me and I'll say *I told you so.*"

5

His apartment is small, not much bigger than a room at his uncle's motel. It is bare, cold, impersonal. There is nothing upon the grey walls, no photographs, no paintings, no decoration. It is like Sonia's place, though it does not appear lived in, there is no warmth, no ageing in the walls or the furniture here. Unlike Sonia, he has a television. Sometimes he will sit alone on the sofa opposite, watch it, its glow the only light in the room, throwing his shadow back large on the wall behind him. He will turn and watch his shadow, watch how it dances with the changing of each scene.

Sonia has never visited this place. No one has. No family, no friends. The people down the hall, his neighbours, they do not know him and he does not know them. He likes it that way. They live the nine-to-five, they keep different hours. Only once have they passed and had occasion to say *Hello*. They were a young couple, the girl a blonde and the boy a brunette. The boy wore dirty clothes and torn jeans to go to work, left a smell like car oil in his wake, probably a mechanic. The girl wore a white blouse and black pencil skirt, flat-soled pumps. A secretary maybe, her hair tied back in a bun where she could secret pens and pencils like a Geisha's chopsticks.

Martin's bedroom holds a single bed that has not been slept on in a long time. It is smartly made, the blankets tight as a drum like he if he was in the army. Again, in this room, there are no pictures. There is dust.

Martin watches a movie on the television. It is a Western. Cowboys and Indians. He watches an Indian drop from a tree branch, drag a cowboy from his horse and pin him to the ground, on his front. The horse bolts. The Indian pulls back the cowboy's head, presses the sharp edge of his knife to the top of his forehead and scalps him. Blood splashes the Indian's face, his bared teeth, mingles with his war paint. The Indian stands, takes the scalp, his prize. The cowboy thrashes and screams on the ground, the top of his skull showing through all the red. The camera stays on him for a long time. His screams become white noise.

To Martin's left, the window, there is a flash, like a camera. He turns to the window. It doesn't happen again.

He stands and presses himself to the glass and looks down at the street. A man walks away, alone, a dark shape with the hood of his jacket pulled up over his head. It might be Joensen.

6

Auntie Marge has made lasagne.

"I saved you some," she says. "You don't look like you're eatin."

Martin sees the plate, the mess of pasta and meat and sauce that looks as though it belongs in a dog's bowl, and feels his stomach churn. "Thank you," he says.

"You wanna heat it up, just come through and use the microwave. You won't disturb us." When Auntie Marge speaks, the fat beneath her chin shakes.

"Thank you."

She steps back but doesn't leave. "You spoke to your mother recently?"

He nods. "Yeah." It is a lie.

"You have?" She sounds pleased, though her face doesn't change. "How is she?"

"She's fine. She said to say hello, to you and Howie." Another lie, one Auntie Marge might see through. Her sister, Martin's mother, despises her brother-in-law. She thinks he is sleazy, a slug, and hates the fact her sister is married to him, and that her son works for him.

"That's nice. Next time you talk to her, you tell her I asked how she was doin."

"Okay."

Auntie Marge leaves, goes through the door at the back of the reception that leads into her house. The door closes but does not lock. Martin stares at the lasagne plate until he can feel his throat begin to crawl. He takes it outside, dumps it in the bushes for the strays and the rats.

Night is longer than day. He flicks through a magazine. He watches the motel through the glass. Minutes crawl by. No one is going to check in to the motel. No one ever does. Not at night. He goes outside, leans against the wall, looks up at the stars. The sky is clear. In the distance, a coyote howls. A dog barks. A woman screams. A man laughs. Noises, indistinguishable, arriving from different points in the town to meet up in the sky and become as one, one source, one beginning and end, as if they have all issued from the same misshapen creature.

Closer, Martin can hear music. One of the rooms upstairs, not far from sixteen where two men wait their turn. Music heavy and electronic, a menacing beat underscored by electric screeches accompanied by a woman's voice softly singing, as though she belongs to a different song. Martin closes his eyes, breathes deeply. The air is warm still, but it will soon cool. He listens to the music. It sounds like it will never end. The noise of it fades inside his head, he becomes deaf to it, and he feels like he is somewhere else.

Somewhere good.

The park, cleaned and made right by a bunny.

Sonia's room, with her, inside her.

In his apartment, alone. Everything quiet, everything still.

Alone.

Peace.

The song ends and he can hear again. Something else begins to play. A man sings now, though the music remains as abrasive. His voice is a growl, a bark, something animal. It belongs in the song. It is not the ethereal whisper of the woman.

A door opens. He looks. Room twenty. The drug dealer's room. Figures, tall and thin and dark, file out, spread out, stumble side to side. Five of them. The one in the lead makes it out onto the car park's asphalt and stops, looks up to the sky, stays there, neck craned. The others stagger up alongside him, do the same. They watch the sky. From the room they have exited, the door is pushed closed, slammed shut.

They stand like statues, frozen, no movement, no sound. They look like they've fallen asleep standing, turned to the stars, or they've taken root, growing towards the moonlight. A dog, a stray, emerges from the darkness surrounding the motel and steps into the pool of flickering light where the men are, heads towards them, its claws scratching on the hard ground. It sniffs at their feet, their legs. It raises a hind and pisses on one of them. It sniffs the air, looks to Martin, comes over to him. Martin holds out his hand and it licks his fingers, then it turns and goes to the bushes, to the food he has dumped there, and it eats.

The men remain turned to the stars, transfixed. Martin goes back inside, takes his seat behind the counter. He looks at the little television, thinks about turning it on, but doesn't. He looks outside, through the glass, at the motel and the broken lamps and the darkness, into the darkness most of all, the wilderness there. There could be anything, out there, looking back at him. He turns off the lamp and sits in the dark. The wild becomes no clearer. He can hear cars, distant, the growling engines of lorries passing through.

During the night, during the very early morning, a point comes when the world is finally still, or as close as it ever gets. The smokers on the balcony are at a minimum, there is maybe one man waiting to get into room sixteen, there are no men in the car park and no animals passing through, and the cars on the highway are few and far between. The darkness is almost absolute, as if it has spread across the globe, encroaching upon this last small patch of flickering light, to engulf it, to consume. At that hour, everything will be so calm, serene. There is peace. It does not last long. Minutes, sometimes just seconds, but it always comes, and Martin always knows it, and sits and embraces it, sits and listens to the nothingness and looks out at the nothingness until finally a car will pass, or a smoker will cough, or a gust of wind will rattle the window in its frame.

These are the moments that make the night worthwhile. The moments that make the motel feel as though it is not just out on the edge of the town, but that it is teetering on the brink of the abyss, threatening to drop off into oblivion, and suddenly it doesn't feel like such a bad place to be. In these moments everything disappears, as if it has never been.

That moment has not yet arrived. Not on this night. Not while the men remain in the car park, and the wild dog feeds from the bushes.

There is movement at the glass, dark shapes. Martin turns. The men have moved. They stand there, all five of them, they press themselves up against the glass and look in at him. Their faces are pale, like ghosts. Their eyes are empty, and all five pairs look directly at him, but they do not see him. Their mouths hang slack and from one man, maybe two, noises escape, low groans like the pained moans of sick men, though it is impossible to tell from whom the sounds come.

Four of the men move on, one remains at the glass. He sways slightly. He does not try to enter. He stares at Martin and Martin stares back. Beside him there is a sharp cry, the dog. The shocked bark becomes a whimper, then nothing. The man presses a hand flat against the glass, almost a goodbye, then turns and shuffles out of view, follows the others.

Martin stands, goes to the glass and looks out, to the right where the dog was and where the men have gone. The man who was last at the glass is standing still, his back to Martin, but the other four are on their knees, the dog between them, dead and open. They reach into the gaping bloody hole torn in its side with stained hands, and they remove meat, press it to their mouths and eat. Their faces, their pale white faces, are smeared dark with the dog's blood, it drips from their chins, and their cheeks are bearded with its fur.

The fifth man steps around them, his feet drag along the ground. He walks away, out into the darkness where there are no lights in the distance, until it takes him in its embrace, holds him close, and he is gone.

7

"Hold my hand."

Martin takes Sonia's hand, leads her out of her apartment. "How do you feel?" he says.

Sonia takes a deep breath. Her fingers are locked tightly in his, crushing his knuckles and joints. Her chewed fingernails dig bluntly into his palm. "Fine," she says. "I'm fine." She wears denim shorts and cowgirl boots, a denim jacket over a torn Jesus and Mary Chain t-shirt. She's braided different coloured beads into a lock of hair behind her left ear. She wears no feathers.

The thing Sonia has, the thing she doesn't like to call agoraphobia because that isn't quite right, makes her prone to anxiety attacks when she leaves the apartment. Sometimes she is high enough she floats through being outdoors, and sometimes she is so high it makes things worse.

Martin holds her hand. They make their way down the stairs. A syringe crunches under Martin's boot. He scrapes his foot along the ground to get rid of the glass. They pass a man sitting on the stairs. His arms are wrapped around his knees, he wears jeans and a frayed woollen jumper with the sleeves pulled down over his hands. He smiles at them as they pass, his top row of teeth biting in to his bottom lip and Martin thinks he has seen him before.

One floor down, a woman with wild hair passes them. She brushes Sonia's arm and Sonia forces herself closer to Martin. He looks at her and sees she is holding her breath. They say nothing. They take the stairs one step at a time. Sonia holds him tight, concentrates on making her way down. They make it outside, and it is not until they make it down the road, away from the block, that Sonia finally exhales.

"Where are we going?" she says.

"To the park."

"Why?"

"I don't know."

"You don't know."

"I want to get outside."

"Why?"

"It'll be good for you."

"For me?"

"It's suffocating in there."

"That's dramatic."

"I couldn't breathe."

"You could've opened a window."

"It isn't like that."

"Then what is it? In your head?"

"I don't know. What does it matter? Come on."

She walks with him, looks round herself with narrowed eyes that are pained by the light, though it is not a bright day. Clouds hang low, the sun hides from view. Sonia walks slowly. Martin finds his arm trailing behind himself, her fingers still locked tightly with his own. He looks back to see her staring at things with girlish wonder, like she's never seen cars before, or buildings, or a man walking a dog.

She stops then and his arm is wrenched back. He turns. She is looking over the road. She smiles. She raises a hand and waves. There is no one there.

"Who're you waving at?"

"The clown."

There is no clown. There is a diner, and on the side of the diner there is graffiti. A dragon, green and red, orange smoke billows from its nostrils.

"He's blowing bubbles. The bubbles are turning into birds and they're flying, up and away."

"Is he red and green?"

"His face is white and blue. His suit is brown and orange. He's wearing a hat with a red flower in it, but I don't think the flower is real. It looks plastic."

"There is no clown."

She says nothing, then "Maybe you're wrong and I'm right."

"There's a dragon, painted on the bricks."

"I can't see a dragon."

"It's not there either. Not really."

"He's waving at me. He wants me to cross over."

"Come on."

In the park they find a bench to sit on. It is quiet, without children, or mothers pushing babies in their prams. The hot dog vendor is there, he leans against the rusted railing and smokes, looks bored. Sonia asks for one so Martin pays. The vendor does not speak, other than to ask "Onions?" Sonia gets onions.

They sit on the bench. The vendor is nearby but he ignores them. He stares at the sky, watches the clouds.

Sonia eats. She takes her time. Each mouthful is slowly, thoroughly chewed. Halfway through, she gives up. "I'm done," she says. She holds it out. "D'you want it?"

Martin shakes his head.

"You sure?"

"Give it to the birds."

She does. Throws the bun and the dog on the floor and wipes her fingers with the napkin it was wrapped in. It does not take long for birds to arrive, to peck at the food and tear it between themselves until there is nothing left, and still they peck at the smallest of crumbs on the ground.

Sonia belches. "I went to a friend's house the other day," she says.

Martin looks at her. "Does she live in the block?"

"No, but I was having a good day. It was one of those days when I feel like I used to, when we first met. Remember that girl?" She grins. "Some mornings I wake up and I feel like such a fuckin shut-in, such a fuckin *recluse*, that I just need to get up and get out and fuckin *do* somethin."

Martin remembers when they first met. It was early morning, he was coming off a shift at the motel. He passed a bus stop and she was sitting there, an unlit cigarette dangling from her bottom lip, dressed in army-green shorts and a man's shirt with the sleeves rolled up and the hem knotted so her midriff was bare, most of her skin on show though she didn't seem to feel the cold. There was more weight on her then, but still her stomach was toned, the musculature clear. Atop her head half her hair was pink, and the other half was green. The dye had faded and grown out, her roots were showing. She searched her pockets for something. She looked up, saw him, squinted at him through rising dawn. "You got a light?" she said.

"No."

She looked disappointed, clucked her tongue and went back to checking her pockets. She seemed to have a lot of pockets for such little clothing. "I've got a lighter here somewhere."

Martin watched her, wanted to talk to her more, wanted to help her though he couldn't. He looked at the bus timetable, said to her, "There's no bus for another hour."

She raised an eyebrow. "I'm not waiting for a bus."

"Oh."

"I'm just taking a seat, and trying to smoke." She stood. "You going into town?"

"Yeah."

"I'll walk with you." She tucked the cigarette behind her ear. "Reckon there'll be anywhere I can buy a lighter? Somewhere open? Shit, a box of matches will do."

"Somewhere's always open," Martin said.

She laughed. "Someone, somewhere. Wanna find him? Or do you have somewhere you need to be?"

Martin shook his head. "I'm all yours."

She is thinner now. It is as if someone has reached inside and scooped fat and muscle from inside her body, her face, and pulled the skin tight. It is as if someone has reached inside her head, too, and switched round the wires. They used to go out a lot, back then. Just walking, sometimes. They'd walk round town in the early hours in a facsimile of that first meeting, looking to see who, if anyone, was open. If they found someone they'd buy a lighter as a keepsake, or a box of matches. It was a private joke.

Then Sonia would insist they head back to her place. Sometimes she said she didn't want to go walking, she'd feign illness, or tiredness. Then one day she said no. "I can't."

"You can't?"

"I can't."

And told him how she'd left the apartment, and something had hit her hard in the chest like a battering ram, something not there, something that took hold of her and squeezed tight until she couldn't breathe and she'd dropped to her knees, gasping, feeling like she was gonna throw up, like the whole building was spinning and she was gonna pass out but none of these things happened and then she didn't know if she was still kneeling or lying or standing or walking or floating or flying then she's falling down the stairs, falling all the way down for what feels like forever, what it must feel like jumping off the top of a skyscraper, until finally she hits the bottom and she spits blood and her teeth all feel loose and there's a great big bump like a boulder on the top of her head and the building is still spinning, she can't see straight, and she still can't move and she still can't breathe. She lay there for a long time. People passed but no one helped her. When she finally could, she crawled back up the stairs, and it took as long getting back up them as it had falling down them, and she crawled along the hallway back to her apartment, she closed the door and she didn't go out.

"Just sit with me," she said.

So he did.

They are back in the park, on the bench, the bored vendor and the bird-devoured hot dog.

"The TV was on in the background and she had her daughter sitting in front of it, watching it. 'Keeps her quiet,' she says. The kid's about three or four. Eventually she gets up to make a coffee, asks me if I want one, I say okay. She goes off into the kitchen, I'm alone in the room with the kid and the TV. The kid has no interest in me, her back's to me, so I start watching TV over the top of her head. It's a show, a kid's show, with puppets, I think these puppets are supposed to be a family. The dad puppet is on a painted set, made to look like he's in a bar, and he's drinking and smoking, and when he gets home he starts beating the mother puppet. And there're these two kids, one of them's snorting lines of coke and the other's teaching how to roll a blunt. They get high together with this painted background that's done up all psychedelic and it revolves, goes three-sixty in one direction then back again the other. And the kid just sits there and watches it."

"I've never seen it."

"There was a cartoon on right after it. A hippo that when it ate mushrooms it could fly. Then the news. I think it was the news. There was a montage at the beginning. Showed a war being fought somewhere, bombed out buildings in the middle of a desert, women crying and a man with a bloody stump for a left arm and he was screaming. There was a close-up of a tank firing. Then a man that looked like a cat and he was climbing up a tree. Then there was a Ku Klux Klan march. Then my friend brought the coffee and I didn't have to watch it anymore."

A couple of birds, maybe the same ones that ate Sonia's unfinished hot dog, hang around the vendor, watch him like they expect a handout. The vendor stares at them, unfazed. The birds step forward, take their time, like he isn't going to notice, like they can creep all the way up and help themselves. The vendor flicks his cigarette at them. They squawk and fly away.

"I'm never going to get a television," Sonia says. "It's poison. Do you have one?"

"Yeah," he says. "It's poison." He stands. "You coming?"

She takes his hand. "Sure."

They go further into the park. Sonia strides confidently alongside him now, but every so often she will falter, she will take small steps and hesitate. Martin looks at the ground, at the dumped trash. It looks like there is more since he was last here, but the way the wind whips it up and moves it round it is hard to tell. The clean-up the bunny promised has not yet begun. They stop at the water feature. A cherub pouring water. An anarchy A has been painted onto the cherub's stomach and on its head someone has carefully placed a crown of thorns. Martin looks into the water. A black bug swims along on the surface. Below that, pennies shine. Wishes. Martin finds a loose coin in his pocket, throws it in. The splash is small.

"Did you make a wish?"

Martin doesn't answer.

"Don't tell me if you did," Sonia says quickly. "Keep it to yourself. If you tell, it might not come true. Like blowing out all the candles on a birthday cake."

Martin can feel eyes. He peers round the water feature, sees a cowboy sat on a bench, a cigarette at his lips. On the ground at his feet there are many dumped and crushed butts, like he's been chain smoking. His clothes are old and faded, torn and tattered. The headband of his hat is yellow with sweat. He looks back at Martin, nods, then raises the hand holding the cigarette in a wave. It is the bunny.

"This has been nice," Sonia says.

Martin grunts.

"I'm ready to go home."

They leave the cherub, the bunny dressed as a cowboy, make their way from the park. Martin looks back without stopping. The cowboy stands. He dumps the cigarette, lights a new one, goes to the water feature and puts his arm into it, scoops out a handful of coins, puts them soaking wet into his pocket. He does it again. Does it until both pockets are full and heavy and dripping. He sees Martin watching. He waves again.

8

There are three kids, teens, they giggle in a darkened corner of the shop. They wear a uniform of loose jeans and backward-facing baseball caps, basketball jerseys and high-top sneakers. They flick through magazines they are never going to buy and snigger at what they find inside, schoolboys in a place too young to enter, looking at things they shouldn't. On the wall beside the door there is a sign, NO MINORS. They have ignored it, and sometimes Joensen will ignore his own rule provided the minors are prepared to purchase something and pretend to be over eighteen.

Martin is at the till. The kids were here before he was. They don't interest him. He watches the naked bounce-dancing Monroe. She watches him. Joensen is beside them both. He watches the kids in the corner, makes sure they don't secret anything down their baggy jeans. One of the three, the boy in the middle of the huddle, fair skin pimpled and his chin badly scraped and spotted with blood where he's been picking the scab, peers back over his shoulder, sees Joensen watching them, turns back to his friends. His shoulders hunch, he whispers, they all laugh.

Joensen nudges Martin with his elbow. "I've got something to show you," he says. He talks to Martin out the corner of his mouth. He wheezes. "I'll get it when they're gone."

Martin knows it will be a photo. He glances in the direction of the kids.

"I think they're settled." He notices that the tallest of the three, stood on the right, has his hand in his pocket, and that it is doing more than playing with loose change.

Joensen clears his throat. "You boys planning on buying anything?" he says.

The boy on the left answers. "Could be," he says. "We just gotta find the right thing we're lookin for, is all."

"You're lookin for somethin specific?"

"We'll know it when we see it." He flashes a big grin, shows all his teeth, then turns back to the magazine.

The kid on the right begins to groan.

"We don't stock anything with girls your age," Joensen says.

The speaker doesn't turn. "Yeah, sure you don't."

"We'd get in a lot of trouble if we did."

"Be cool, man – we're the right age."

Joensen nudges Martin again, smiles at him with a wicked glint in his eye, then ducks below the counter, thumbs through the stock kept there. He stands, a thin magazine rolled in one meaty fist like he is planning to swat a fly, then rounds the counter and approaches the group, opens it to the centrefold, and dumps it over what they are looking at. "This to your taste?"

"What the fuck, man!" the kid on the left says.

The middle boy with the scraped chin chokes out a cry, backs off.

The kid on the right groans louder, but now it sounds like he is going to be sick.

They step away, make for the door. "Fuck you, man!" the kid on the left, the group's spokesperson, says. "That's sick! You're fucked up!"

Joensen waves them out the door. "Bye-bye, now!"

Joensen puts the magazine they were flicking through back in the rack, then brings the other back to the till, puts it away. Martin sees the cover. It is entitled *BLA*. He knows this stands for *Beast Lovers Anonymous*. The woman on the front is crouched behind a sitting dog. The dog is leaning back to lick her chin. The woman has blonde hair and wears glasses, stares out from the cover with narrowed *Fuck-me* eyes and the tip of her tongue pokes out from the corner of her open mouth. The anonymity of the men and women inside is preserved with black bars across their eyes. No names are given within the publication, every piece of correspondence on the letters page is signed from *Anon*, and information on meet-ups is provided in code. Joensen gets down on one knee to put it back, a subscription copy they hold for a regular customer.

"Do you wanna see this month's centrefold?" he says. He grins.

Martin looks away.

Joensen stands, waddles over to his desk and returns with a photograph. He holds it out for Martin to see, the newest spectacle of his amateur photographic endeavours. "Look at her eyes," he says. "Hasn't she got the fucking *saddest* eyes you've ever seen?"

The girl does have sad eyes. She has pale skin and long brown hair that hangs straight down either side of her head. The picture is of her face, zoomed in on, nothing else. Her eyes are brown and the skin around them is dark. She is looking straight into the camera.

"Did she see you?"

"It's just really well-timed, you believe it? I mean, she mighta had an idea after I took the picture, but by then I was gone. It's perfect. I wasn't gonna get a better shot than that. You know what else?" He sounds like he is about to boast. "I only had *this much* space between her curtains to get that shot." He holds up his thumb and index finger less than an inch apart.

Martin looks at the picture, held by those haunted eyes.

"You know where I'm going to put her? She's not going on the wall, she's going on the ceiling, right above my bed. Every morning when I wake up, I'm going to be staring straight into those eyes. And every night, when I go to sleep, I'll go looking into them. She's beautiful. Don't you think?"

"Yeah," Martin says. "Very beautiful."

"You know where she lives?"

"Where?"

"The trailer park. You believe that? All those hicks, and here's this girl, looks like she belongs in a French movie."

"You need to be careful, going there. If they catch you."

"They won't catch me."

"I'm sure everyone says that, right before they're caught."

Joensen laughs. "If I turn up one day sporting two black eyes and missing a few teeth, then you can tell me you told me so." He puts away the picture of the sad-eyed girl.

"They'll do more than knock out a few teeth."

Joensen snorts. "How do you know so much about it?"

Martin shrugs. "I've heard things."

"We've all heard things, doesn't make it true."

Martin looks at the picture again, looks at it for a long time, studies it. It is perfect. It makes his chest tight. Her eyes stare right back into his. "If you get caught, will you stop?"

Joensen shrugs. "Guess we won't know til we know, right?"

The door opens. A woman enters. She is thin, has long black hair, a black dress decorated with white pentagrams. She is a regular, though Martin doesn't know her name. She nods at them and they nod back, then she goes through the beaded curtain into the next room.

Martin motions after her. "Is she on your wall?"

"Probably," Joensen says. "Somewhere."

The door opens again. A midday rush. Two men enter, maybe together, maybe not. They don't talk. One goes to the magazines, the same corner that was earlier occupied by the three boys, and the other goes to the DVD's.

Joensen takes the picture of the sad-eyed girl, returns her to a safe place in one of the drawers of his desk. He returns to the counter, snaps his fingers like he's remembered something, then reaches into his pocket. "Hey, I've got another one here. Took this a coupla nights ago. It's a couple shot.

Two for the price of one, huh?"

The picture is Aunt Marge, naked, her sagging body having long succumbed to gravity every inch of her grey flesh hangs down. She is on her bed, her weight on one knee and her other leg raised, preparing to mount a naked Howie, his penis engorged and held steady, pointing into the darkness below her waist.

Martin grabs the picture, tears it up, dumps it in the trash.

"What the fuck?" Joensen says. He looks shocked.

Martin glares. "Don't fuck with me," he says.

9

The television is old, plays in grainy black and white. Martin glances at it intermittently, and when he looks up to peer over the counter towards the glass door he is momentarily blind, dark spots dance before his eyes.

He watches it muted. On the screen, two men beat a third. He is on the ground. One of the standing men has a hammer. He beats the fallen man with it, smashes his knees and his elbows. The man screams silently, the camera closes in on his face, the black void of his open mouth. The hammer breaks his fingers, his hands, his wrists. The man tries to crawl away, wriggles his torso, his stomach and chest scrape the ground. He moves by inches. The man with the hammer places a boot in the centre of his back, holds him in place. The other standing man has a gun. He kneels beside the fallen man, takes a handful of his hair and presses the barrel to the back of his head. It stays there for a long time. The victim looks like he is begging for his life. Finally, the gun fires. The bullet tears through the back of his skull, blows off the front of his face. The head flops forward. There is a pool of blood, getting bigger. The two men, the torturer and the killer, they step back, closer to the camera, turn to it. One holds the bloodied hammer, the other the gun. They smile into the camera, smile at Martin.

He goes to the door but does not open it. Looks out at the car park through the glass. There are dogs, five of them. They sit in the dim glow cast by the streetlamps. A sixth enters the circle of light from the surrounding darkness. A seventh. A gathering of them. Wild dogs, collarless, coming from the dark nothing, the encroaching nowhere. They sit, sniff the ground, take a few idle paces in one direction and then the next. Martin watches them, half-expects them to raise their heads to the sky as one and begin to howl, but they don't.

Before long they have filled the car park, a mass of ragged, mangy fur. They sit silent below the flickering lights. Men smoking on the balcony watch them, do not try to disperse them. They finish their cigarettes and go back inside. Some of the dogs look at Martin. They sit in front of the glass door and look up at him with sad dog eyes.

In the morning, with the coming of the dawn, they will be gone. He is sure of it. When the sun rises, they will leave, as if they've never been here at all.

In the morning, they will be gone.

The dogs.

In the morning, the dogs will be gone.

Martin places his hands upon the glass, lowers himself onto his haunches to be of a height with the dogs watching him. Their eyes follow him down. He presses his forehead against the cool glass. He looks back at them.

10

"Hey." Sonia is high. She gives him a dreamy smile with closed eyes, sways where she stands holding the door open, her hand on the lever all that keeps her upright.

Martin closes the door, holds her by an elbow and leads her to the sofa. "How are you?" he says.

"I'm just dandy." Her eyes are still closed. She manages to open the left, turn it on him briefly, then closes it again. She hums to herself.

"Looks like you've gotten an early start."

"Early. Late. Maybe I've never stopped. I'll just keep going."

"If you don't fall asleep first."

She gets both eyes open. "Asleep? I'm wide awake. I could bounce all night." Her lids slowly droop, close. She bites the corner of her lip, then starts giggling to herself.

"What's funny?"

"Huh?"

"Nothing."

Sonia draws a leg up and sits on it, rests the side of her face against the sofa, wraps her fingers round her bare knee. She wears a summer dress though it is not summer, a thin white one that falls just below her waist and is held up by two straps that cut into her shoulders.

It looks like she is falling asleep. Her breathing gets slower, her lips part, slack, her body goes limp.

"Sonia," Martin says.

She gives a start.

"Are you sleeping?"

She laughs.

"What have you taken?"

She mumbles something.

"How do you feel?"

She grunts.

Martin leaves her alone. He sits back, clasps his hands, listens to her shallow breathing, the small snores that gargle in the back of her throat. For a long time, he listens to her breathe. He puts his hand on her chest, palm flat against her ribs, and he feels her heartbeat. It is weak, but it is regular. He stands, picks her up in his arms. She does not stir. He is not strong but she is not heavy. He carries her through to the bedroom, lies her down upon her bed, on top of the covers. He doesn't pull the blanket over her because it isn't cold.

The curtain in her room is drawn. He opens it, looks down. Sonia's apartment is at the back of the building. Below, there is a patch of dead earth. Some children play on it, kick a ball between themselves, bounce it off a wheel-less and rusted shopping trolley. A woman lies on the grass, legs and midriff bare, like she is sunbathing though the sky is filled with clouds.

Martin goes into the adjoining bathroom. He leaves the curtain open. The light from outside is weak and Sonia does not stir. He takes a piss, washes his hands, then pauses as he dries them, hears something. Movement, footsteps. Someone is in the apartment. He tries to remember if he locked the door after he came in, but he doesn't think he did, preoccupied with keeping Sonia upright.

The bathroom door is open slightly, he peers out through the narrow gap. A man enters the bedroom. Martin recognises him – the man from the staircase, the man sat with his arms wrapped round his knees, smiling up at him, at them. He wears the same clothes, but he isn't smiling now. He bites his lip, stares at Sonia intently. He rounds the bed, leans over her, gets close to her face. Sniffs her. She doesn't flicker, doesn't wake. He breathes in the smell of her face, her hair, her neck. Reaching out, he strokes her cheek with one curled finger.

He goes to the foot of the bed. He moves slow, like a cat in the night, stalking. His teeth are still in his lip. A trickle of blood runs from the corner of his mouth, down his chin. He raises the hem of her short dress, peels off the white panties there, drops them. He undoes his pants, climbs onto the bed, on top of Sonia.

Martin turns away.

The bedsprings creak. The man grunts. Sonia makes no sound. Martin grits his teeth. He catches sight of himself in the mirror above the sink. He looks away. The man starts to make a choked sound like a pig being slaughtered.

When the creaking stops he looks back into the room. The man crawls slowly from the bed, does himself up. His teeth aren't in his lip anymore, his mouth hangs open, his jaw slack. His chin is smeared red. He backs out of the room, his eyes still on Sonia. Martin hears him leave, hears the door click slowly closed, then silence. The man didn't look through the apartment, investigate her other rooms. He had no interest in them.

Martin leaves the bathroom, crosses the floor, rounds the bed, slowly, like the man did. Sonia makes strange noises. Something runs from the corners of her mouth, something yellow-white and foamy. Her body convulses. Her lips are turning blue. She has thrown up. She is choking.

Martin watches her. He watches her choking, turning blue, dying. Her body shakes, though with less intensity than it earlier had. She does not wake. Her body's struggle grows weaker. She fades. She grows still.

Martin rolls her onto her side, rubs her back. Vomit falls from her mouth, onto the blanket. Mostly bile, it runs, drips off the side of the bed and onto the toes of his boots. Sonia begins to cough, then wheeze, then gasp. Finally, her breathing settles into a rhythm, though for a long time there is a harshness to it, until finally it is calm and steady, peaceful, like it was before.

She does not wake.

11

It is raining. Martin sits alone in the park, clothes soaked through, his hair clings to the side of his face and lies flat against his scalp. The park is empty, almost, no hot dog vendor, no bunny or cowboy, no kids. Just a woman that paces the footpaths dressed in a black robe that clings to her in the wet. A green witch mask obscures her face, a Halloween disguise. On her feet she wears yellow rubber boots and she kicks at the puddles of rain. Sometimes she jumps in them, makes a big splash, and laughs.

Someone has drawn a Groucho Marx moustache on the cherub, and the thick-rimmed spectacles to match. A condom hangs from one hand, maybe used.

The sky is dark. It is the middle of the day but it feels like it is almost night time. Thunder rumbles in the distance behind him. The rain intensifies. The woman in the black dress and witch mask laughs harder and runs fast circles round the water feature, arms up in the air, waving. Martin watches the rain splash on top of the water, like a dance upon the surface. Despite the disruption, he can still see the coins at the bottom, the way some of them shine.

Wishes.

Loose change.

Wishes.

Loose change, emptied from pockets, no use.

Wishes.

Pennies.

The witch stops running, catches her breath at a railing on the other side of the feature. She presses her back to it, looks at Martin, does a double-take as if seeing him for the first time. It is hard to read her reaction through the mask. Her eyes are in darkness, two black hollows in amongst all the green skin and the brown warts.

She approaches him. Walks slowly through the rain, like she is making her way down a catwalk. Martin watches her out the corner of his eye, ignores her until she is three paces away, where she stops, stands, waits for him to see her. He turns. The masked face is cocked to one side. He can see the eyes now, blue, unblinking.

They look at each other, do not speak. The green rubber face is unchanging.

The witch reaches down then, takes the hem of her dress in both hands and raises it until it is higher than her waist, her naked crotch exposed. She has a penis, it hangs limp against the inside of her leg, the whole area milky pale and shaved smooth. She drops the dress then turns and runs away, splashes through the puddles as she goes. She laughs. The sound is girlish to Martin's ears.

He stands and goes to the water, reaches in and pulls out a coin. It probably isn't his, the one he threw in, but it will do. He puts it in his pocket and leaves.

12

He is supposed to be behind the desk, waiting for check-ins that will never come, but he isn't. He stands outside room twenty, knocks on the door. Waits a long time and receives no answer. Knocks again. Is about to knock a third time when the door opens.

The drug dealer answers, pokes his head out, looks Martin up and down, seems to recognise him. His face turns mean. He probes the inside of a cheek with his tongue. "There a problem?"

"No."

The dealer frowns. "Then what the fuck do you want?"

"Can I come in?"

The dealer wears a red cap at an angle. He knocks it forward as he scratches behind his ear, but quickly repositions it. "Why? You think you're gonna find somethin?"

"I hope so."

"Hey man, I pay my rates –"

"I'm not looking to throw you out."

"Oh." The dealer straightens up but remains wary. "That so."

"That's so."

"Then what do you want? Be specific now, my man, I need to hear you say the words. I know what entrapment is, don't be treatin me like no fool and thinkin that I don't."

"I want to get high."

The dealer grins. "Then shit," he opens the door wide, "come on in."

Martin glances at the reception. He's left the lamp on. Aunt Marge and Howie never check in on him. They will never know he's gone. He enters room twenty.

The room is lit by a red bulb that hurts the eyes and there is a potent stink hanging in the air that doesn't so much infiltrate the nostrils as attack them. The drug dealer takes a seat in the corner, on a leather-backed swivel chair. He is alone in the room. Other than the red cap, he wears a white vest and baggy jeans, scuffed sneakers. His arms are incredibly thin. Martin can see the track marks at the inside of each elbow, and the bruises. "So what brings you round?" he says.

"I already told you."

"You've never had occasion to visit before. Take a seat, get comfortable – you in some kinda rush?"

There is a wooden chair in the corner, the varnish faded and the legs weak. Martin sits on it cautiously. "There's no rush," he says. "And there's no reason."

The dealer smiles. "Bullshit. Somethin as abrupt as this, there's gotta be a reason. But I ain't gonna pry, man, be easy. You wanna keep it to yourself then you go right ahead and keep it to yourself. I'm Rodansky, by the way." He holds out his hand.

Martin shakes it, gives his name.

"Martin, huh? Always wondered. We see you sometimes, at that desk, fuckin glow-in-the-dark you're so pale. *Martin*. I'll have to let Joanie know. You know what she calls you?"

"Who's Joanie?"

"The girl-next-door up in room sixteen."

The whore. "I've never met her."

"Well, you'd never met me before tonight, but we always been aware of each other. Give it time. Anyway, what was I sayin? Oh yeah – you know what she calls you? *The Vampire*. On account a your complexion. And that we only ever see you at night." Rodansky grins. "That why you're here really? You here to drink my blood?"

"Let's not rule anything out just yet."

Rodansky laughs. "What's your flavour, man? You name it, I'll see if I can accommodate."

"I don't have a flavour. I don't care. Just give me something that'll take me somewhere else."

Rodansky blinks. "*Shiiiiit*. Gimme a second, let me see what I can rustle up." He stands, goes into the bathroom. Martin hears things being moved round, clattering.

The bed is unmade, the blanket in a heap on the floor and the sheets dishevelled, loose from the mattress, and stained with what looks like every bodily fluid. At the foot of the bed, on top of the cabinet there, the television is on, but it plays nothing. Just static.

Rodansky comes back. He almost trips on the wheel of his leather swivel chair but rights himself and kicks it to one side. The chair looks like it belongs under a desk with a computer on top of it, but there is no such desk here. He brings Martin a small cup, the kind given to old folk in nursing homes, filled with their meds. This one holds meds, too. Multicoloured little pills that look like candy.

"What is it?" Martin says.

"A cocktail," Rodansky says. "Are you sitting comfortably?"

"How much do you want?"

"Take that hand outta your pocket, man. We're all friends here."

Martin throws back the cup, swallows the pills. Rodansky squeezes his thigh and climbs back into the nearby chair.

"I'll see you when you get back," he says.

Martin settles in. He watches the static on the television. He can see shapes in it, faces. "I'm not a vampire," he says.

"Shit, even your uncle says it. Joanie told me."

"He's not my uncle."

"Whatever. It's cos you're pale man, that's all. You're very pale."

"I can't remember the last time the sun shone."

"Neither can I."

"It always looks like it's going to rain. Then sometimes it does rain."

"I stay indoors. There's nothing outside for me."

Martin nods slowly. "No, you're right," he says. "There's nothing out there for anyone. Nothing at all."

"Beyond those lights, the world is ending."

"It feels that way."

"You hear that shit they say on TV sometimes, in the movies – that the world is a good place? You ever hear that?" Rodansky laughs. "Bull, man. Don't believe a fuckin word of it. I can see you don't, you're like me. You don't listen to their lies, don't swallow what you're spoonfed. Fuck, you've just gotta look outta your damn window to see what kinda world we all live in, am I right?"

He keeps talking, but his voice grows smaller and smaller, tunes out, until finally it sounds as though it is coming from far away, from another room, through a wall. There is a noise like the sea in Martin's ears, his blood rushing, pounding, building to a roar.

Then silence.

Martin looks round the room. Rodansky is gone. In his place, upon his chair, sits the man from Sonia's building. He sits up straight, his hands rest on his knees. He smiles at Martin with his teeth in his lip. Blood runs down his chin. It pools at his feet. He grinds his jaw side to side and his teeth cut deeper and it makes a sound like a saw cutting through wet meat.

The television is off, the screen blank. The light is regular, not red, the room dimly lit by a dying bulb. The bed is made. Everything is as it should be, the way the room would have looked on its first day, virgin, before it took its first occupant.

There is a scratching sound to Martin's left. Nothing there. Smoke rises from under the bathroom door. The scratching gets louder. Insects begin to crawl down the wall, across the carpet. They cover the wall, turn it into a seething black mass, so many they look like one creature, a living thing, breathing. There is a face in it.

A dog barks. Martin looks. Everything moves slow-motion. It feels like he is underwater. The man is gone from Rodansky's chair. The chair is gone and, instead, there is a dog in the centre of the room. It looks back at him. Its mouth is moving. Either it is smacking its lips or it is talking. Martin can't hear what it says over the scratching. He tries to lean forward, to get closer, but he can't move. The dog's mouth keeps moving. Its stomach is open. Its entrails hang down, lie in a heap on the ground beneath it. He can see its ribs, broken, they poke jagged through the ripped flaps of its underside, its fur matted with gore.

There is movement at the end of the room, beyond the dog, almost hidden by the smoke. There is a girl there, her back to him. She is naked. She dances. It is Sonia.

The dog comes to him, licks his fingers. Its tongue marks his hand with blood. It looks up at him. It has eyes like a man. It says something to him. It sounds French. He doesn't understand.

13

The man sits on the stairs. His clothes haven't changed, a tatty jumper still pulled down to cover his hands, his arms wrapped around his knees.

Martin stands at the foot of the stairs. Their eyes meet, lock. Where the man sits their faces are level. The man smiles at him. If Martin didn't know better he'd think the man has never moved, carefully positioned like a garden ornament. Like a gargoyle.

Martin starts up the stairs. The man's smile never falters. Martin watches him as he passes, but the man does not turn his head. Martin makes it to the next landing, stops. He goes back down, all the way to the bottom, until their faces are level again. The man does not look surprised to see him return. The smile never wavers, the eyes never blink.

Neither of them speaks a word. Their eyes are locked again. Minutes pass. No one approaches, no one passes. All is still, silent.

"Hello," Martin says.

The man nods, just slightly, the barest tilt of his head.

There is another long silence. Martin grits his teeth. His jaw aches. He looks the man over, notes his poorly shaved head, his sallow skin and sunken eyes. There is a sore at the corner of his mouth, hidden by his constant smile.

"Do you live in this building?" Martin says.

No words, just another nod, and the smile.

"Show me."

The smile falters a little but does not fade, the man tilts his head to the side a little.

"Are you mute?"

No response.

"Show me where you live."

The man stands, comes down the steps and heads along the corridor. Martin follows. They walk for a long time. The walls are marked with spray paint, arrows giving directions to nowhere. There are other images, but they pass them too fast to see what they are. There are no windows. The lights flicker and dim. They pass through darkness, then duck through a broken door, its top half smashed, gone. They go into a room. It might be the man's room. This door hangs from its hinges. There are windows here, but they are covered with thin blankets nailed into place. They let in enough light, dim as it is, and the corner of one blanket billows where Martin can see the window has been smashed with a stone, the shards of broken glass still lying on the ground below, some of it crunched into powder. A cold wind blows.

The apartment is the same layout as Sonia's, but the walls have graffiti scrawled over them and the floor is bare and hard concrete. There is no furniture. Martin follows the man into what should be the bedroom. There is no bed. A rat chews trash in the corner. The man stops, turns, holds out his arms, palms up, to show that this is where he lives.

The damn smile never leaves his face.

"Sit down," Martin says.

The man does. No protest, no questions, no change in his face or demeanour. He does as he is told.

"Lie down."

Martin stands over him. He looks down for a long time. The man looks back at him, doesn't move. His fingers are laced upon his stomach.

Martin raises a boot, holds it above the man's face, carefully positions it. The man raises his eyes to see it. Martin brings the boot down hard in the centre of the man's face. His nose crunches and his teeth smash and the back of his head bounces on the hard floor with a crack. The man jerks and spits blood and teeth and Martin stomps on him again. He teeters with the force of the blow and takes a step back, steadies himself. The man lies very still. The sound of his breathing is as bad as Joensen's asthmatic wheeze. There is a gurgling sound coming from the back of his throat. Martin can see blood trickling slowly from the back of his head. When his eyes flicker open, he can see that the whites are pink, bloodshot. It's hard to tell, his lips mangled, if he is still smiling. Martin raises his boot one last time, takes careful aim, then brings it down as hard as he can. Shock waves ripple through his leg. He steps back, sits down and waits, watches until the man stops breathing.

Sonia smiles. "Hey," she says.

"Hello." Martin takes a seat.

"Where've you been? Haven't seen you in a while."

He says nothing, and when he doesn't respond Sonia pokes her head into his line of sight, waves her hand in front of his face.

"You in there?"

"I'm here."

"Where've you been?"

"Just...busy."

"Oh yeah? Doing what?"

"Work."

"You work too hard, Martin. You ever gonna spend some of that money?"

"If I ever find something to spend it on."

"Shit, can't be that hard. People do it every day." She gets up and messes around in the kitchen, gets herself a drink. "You want anything?"

"Blood."

"What?"

"I'm fine."

She comes back, sits next to him. She isn't high. She seems clear and lucid and pleased to see him. "I went to see my friend yesterday, the one with the kid? I'm getting better, right? Hell," she blows a raspberry, waves her hand, "this outdoor thing doesn't seem like such a big deal anymore. Hey, one day soon you might have to take me out for a real date, the way we used to, remember? Spend some of your money that way. Spend some of it on me." She smiles brightly. She has feathers in her hair and she looks very beautiful.

Martin looks out the window. The clouds hang so low it's like they are right on the other side of the glass.

"You okay?"

"I'm okay."

"I bet you're tired."

"Could be."

She shuffles closer, strokes the side of his face, runs a hand back through his hair and along his shoulder, down his arm. She squeezes his thigh, runs her fingers along the inside of it.

Martin stands. Sonia looks surprised. Her eyes narrow. "Hey, you wanna tell me what's wrong?"

He goes to her bedroom and lies on the bed, covers his face with his arm. Sonia follows. She says his name softly. He doesn't answer.

She climbs onto the bed next to him, lies beside him, puts an arm over him. Martin turns, rolls her onto her back and puts his head on her chest.

Sonia strokes his hair. She says something but he doesn't hear. The side of his face is pressed against her ribcage, he listens to the feathery beating of her heart. It is a faint music, but it is there, he can hear it, it is all he can hear. He listens to it for a long time.

The Shoot

The girl braces herself against the cold, wraps thin arms clad in a threadbare cardigan tightly round herself, lowers her face from the wind. It is dark, late, the streets mostly empty. Cars pass on the road, a couple slow to check her out, thinking maybe she is a hooker. Any other night she'd maybe indulge them, it wouldn't be the first time and it is easy enough to do, usually doesn't take very long, but she has somewhere to be. Could almost say she has 'business'. She is getting paid. He said he will pay her. That is 'business' enough.

Her legs are cold, the air biting at her exposed flesh. She'd asked what she should wear, but he'd said it didn't matter. She's made an effort anyway. None of her clothes are particularly nice, most of them are falling apart, but amongst the dirty piles she managed to find a black vest to go with her cardigan, and a short skirt. Down the back of her wardrobe were a pair of knee-high leather boots she didn't know she still had. If she'd known, she'd have sold them a long time ago. They're worth fifty bucks, at least.

There are no mirrors where she lives. There is one in the bathroom, but an ex-boyfriend smashed it with an angry fist a long time ago and it isn't fit for purpose. Most of the glass fell out on impact, and in the middle, where the fist struck, remains a brown smear where the blood dried. Some of the mirror is still on the bathroom floor, kicked to the side, under the toilet and the bathtub, so it can't cut up bare feet. The only way she can see her reflection is if she is prepared to stoop down and twist her face this way and that to get an impression of how she appears in one of the tiny broken shards. Usually she just doesn't bother.

Despite this, she has an idea of how she looks. Her skin is ghostly pale, she knows this, for she never goes outside during the day and she need simply look at her arms to see what colour she is. Her hair is black, cropped short to just below her jaw, self-cut, and she has bangs that are starting to get a little too long, strands poking into her eyes. With the pale skin, the dark hair and clothes, she knows she must look very goth. Maybe it's a look that works for her. Back in high school she'd always been an outcast, maybe not a goth *per se*, but she'd always been a loner, always kept to herself, wore dark clothes whenever she could, ate her lunch alone on the bleachers in the absence of friends.

Clothes. Fashion. She can't understand why it seems so important to her now, when it has never mattered before.

It's because she is nervous. Because she is hungry, and not for food. There is an itch beginning, under her skin. It has been too long. He's promised her medicine too, as well as the money. In the meantime she needs something to focus on, to keep her mind occupied. Clothes. Clothing.

High school wasn't that long ago. Four years maybe, but it is always so hard to remember how much time has really passed. Everything is a blur. Just her and her mother, back then. Just the two of them, daddy had run away a long time ago. That old chestnut – *Hey hon? I'm just goin out for a pack of cigarettes, you want anythin?* Didn't matter what she wanted, he never came back. At first she'd held tight to a fantasy, and maybe her mother had too, that something had happened to her father and he was every day battling his way back to them, that one day he would return, scarred and rugged, with stories to tell of where he had been and what he had done, and how only his love for the both of them had kept him going. Her grip on this fantasy loosed over time, and eventually she let go of it altogether.

They didn't have much money. What little they did went on bills and food, the latter of which there never seemed to be enough. Her mother worked three jobs, was rarely home and never seemed to sleep. The girl had an after school job too, and another on the weekends. After school she cleaned in an office block downtown, on the weekends she was a checkout girl in the local market.

Their clothes were hand-me-downs and thrift-store tat. At school she was a few decades too late, her clothing like something the kids all wore in movies from the seventies, the bell-bottom jeans and earthy pullovers with shirt-collars sticking out. When she wasn't ignored, she was teased. She pretended to be deaf to what was said, but she heard it all, and sometimes, out on the bleachers, she would tell herself that a rogue tear rolling down her cheek was from the cold, from the wind, and she'd repeat this even on the calmest days in late spring.

She stops thinking – she's gone too far, that was too much. She shakes herself loose. The clothes don't fucking matter, he's told her they won't matter.

She sees the block where he lives, the address he's given her. A hobo rolls past on the sidewalk, pushing a shopping cart with squeaking wheels, the basket loaded with tinned food and bottles of water, bin-liners filled with clothes, and sitting among it all is a blow-up doll wearing a torn and grey wedding dress. The hobo turns to her as she crosses the road, tips his woollen cap and flashes her a smile of rotten and broken teeth, enclosed within a mouth thick with white stubble. "Evenin, miss," he says.

She says nothing in return, but he doesn't wait for a response, just continues on down the street. She goes to the building's entrance, to the intercom, recalls the number he'd said and pushes the buzzer. While she waits, arms still wrapped around herself, she probes at a scab in the left corner of her mouth with the tip of her tongue. It tastes like blood.

A voice crackles. "Hello?"

She leans in close to speak. "Uh, hello."

"Hi."

"Um, hi."

"Who is this?"

"Oh, sorry – it's, um, it's Sally."

"Sally." He repeats the name. She wonders if he is trying to remember who she is, then a moment later he says "Come on up."

The door buzzes and she pushes through. Up two flights of stairs, he waits for her outside his door. He is round like an uncracked Humpty-Dumpty, with curly blonde hair so thin he looks bald on top. She can hear his laboured breathing before she reaches him, hear the way his wheezing breaths rattle in his chest. He smiles at her. "We haven't met," he says.

"No," Sally says. "We spoke on the phone." She stops when she reaches him, stands apart from him.

He looks her over, seems to be appraising her. "Who gave you my number?"

"Lucy." She begins to fidget, tugs at the cuffs of her cardigan, feels awkward, like she should say something else, explain further. "She said you'd pay to take pictures. And that you supplied the drugs. That you were looking for other girls, she said you told her to give your number to anyone that was interested."

He nods, runs a hand down his mouth. At the corners of his lips there are flakes of dried white spit. "Are you a cop?"

"No."

"If you are, you have to tell me. That's how it works. Besides, I'm not doing anything wrong."

"I didn't say you were."

"Yeah, but if cops don't like you, they'll think of something they can nail you with."

"I'm not a cop."

A door opens on the level above them. The fat man looks toward the sound, then ushers her into his apartment. He closes the door but they go no further. "Roll up your sleeves," he says. "Let me see your arms."

She does as he says. He holds her by the wrists, inspects the track marks on the insides of her elbows, a lot of them old and faded, but most of them not. He nods, satisfied. Outside, whoever had opened the door upstairs passes by, heavy footfalls down the hall, then the stairs.

"Come on in," the fat man says. He leads her into the kitchen. "I'm Joensen."

"Okay."

"You said Sally, right?"

"Yeah."

"Sally. Great. You hungry, Sally?"

She shrugs, though she is not, but a potential free meal should never be refused.

The floor of the kitchen is linoleum, its edges under the counters piled high with food crumbs. There are a few dirty dishes in the sink, but mainly there are takeaway cartons stuffed into paper bags and empty pizza boxes taking up most of the space on top of the counters. In the middle of the room is a round wooden table with two chairs. There is a greasy paper bag on top of the table. Joensen takes a seat, opens the bag and reaches inside. "I went out for burgers. They should still be warm. I've got one here for you, if you want it."

"Thanks."

He spreads his food out on the wrapper it came in, pours the fries out from their box. "Take a seat."

She does, keeps her hands clasped together between her thin thighs. Joensen slides her a wrapped burger. The smell of it turns her stomach, makes her feel ill. "I thought we were, um, going to take pictures."

"We'll get to it," Joensen says. "You got somewhere you need to be?"

"Uh..."

"You're hungry for something else, right?"

"It's been a coupla days."

Joensen looks at her, chews. He breathes through his nose while he eats, but it sounds blocked and every so often he gulps a breath through his mouth, affording a view of the mashed meat, bread, and potato between his jaws. The sight does nothing for her appetite. "Well, you're gonna get it, soon, so just stay cool, okay? Food ain't gonna hurt you, and you look like you could do with some. When'd you eat last?"

"I don't know."

"But you remember your last hit, right? Shit. Eat something, you'll feel better."

Tentatively, under his watchful gaze, she unwraps the burger, holds her breath against the smell of it. She takes a small bite, chews quickly and swallows it down, still holding her breath so she can't taste it. She feels like she is going to gag. Put back on the paper, the exposed burger leaks grease onto its wrapper, oozes juice into the base of the toasted bun. There is no lettuce on the burger, no tomato, but there is processed cheese, and ketchup. Sally feels her vision begin to blur as she looks at it, feels the room begin to spin. "I'm going to be sick," she says.

"Jesus," Joensen says, but he doesn't sound panicked, doesn't move to get up, just keeps shovelling the food into his maw, his cheeks like a hamster's. He speaks around his mouthful of food. "Toilet's down the hall, on the left, the door just before the bedroom."

Shakily, Sally gets to her feet and makes her way down the hall, uses the wall for support. She falls to her knees in front of the bowl, wraps her arms around it and throws up. As the vomit passes her lips she sees that the porcelain is marked with shit stains, that the water in the bottom is piss-yellow. She retches hard, the lump of what little burger she has bitten off is first to vacate her, followed by a lot of bile.

When it has stopped, when her stomach has settled, she pinches the bridge of her nose and clears it, wipes it with the back of her hand, spits, then rises to her feet. The room is still spinning. She flushes the toilet, then steadies herself on the sink, runs the cold water and splashes it over her face, into and around her mouth. She takes deep breaths.

There is a knock at the door. Joensen speaks. "You all right?"

Sally clears her throat. "I'm – I'm fine, it was just, uh... I'm just, I'm not hungry."

"Okay. You all right to go ahead?"

She thinks about the money, about the promised drugs. "Yes." She says it quickly.

"Cool. I take it you're not gonna want the rest of that burger, huh?"

She grits her teeth. "No."

"While you're in there, you might as well take off your clothes. We'll get started when you come out."

"Everything?"

"What was that?"

"Do you want me to take everything off?"

"Yeah. Everything." She hears him leave the door, hears him go back down the hall to the kitchen.

She starts to take off her clothes. As she does so, she catches sight of herself in the mirror over the sink. The glass is smudged where a hand has wiped away condensation after a shower, and there are dried marks that look like the explosions of squeezed pimples, but no one has smashed it with their fist. The reflection is clear.

She is thinner than she thought. This is the first thing she notices. Her face is narrow, all sharp edges, her cheeks so hollow she can see the gaps in her teeth through the almost translucent skin.

The next thing she sees are the sores. She sees the redness of her eyes.

Before she can notice anything else, she looks away. She slides her arms out of the cardigan, dumps it on the floor by the bathtub. She takes off the boots next, the skirt, then the vest, adds them to the pile. The draw of the mirror is strong, but she resists until all her clothes are off. She turns, stands naked before it. She doesn't recognise what she sees.

Like the gaps in her teeth, she can count the ribs she has on show. Her stomach is so drawn in it makes her hips look wide. Her small breasts look empty, loose, her nipples point downward, the space on her chest above them is faintly webbed with veins. She stands on her tip-toes to see more of herself in the mirror, below her waist. Her legs are like twigs, her thighs do not touch at the top where her crotch is covered with a thatch of thick, curly hair, and her knees look bigger than they are, and knobbly.

There are scars, too. And scabs.

The scab at the corner of her mouth is bigger than it feels, and it is oozing. It looks painful. She presses a finger to it, like she could wipe it away. It gives a low throb at her touch. She doesn't know what has caused it. A pimple, or maybe she has just scratched there absently, the same way she's acquired the ones on her wrists and forearms.

She grips the bathroom's door handle, takes a deep breath, leaves the room and finds the bedroom, her bare feet padding along the cold floor.

Joensen is checking his camera. He looks up as she enters, gives her a cursory glance, then returns to what he is doing. Sally stands where she is, runs her right hand up and down her left arm. She feels awkward without her clothes, exposed. She doesn't know where to go, how to stand, what to do with her hands.

The room consists of a double bed stripped down to the mattress, the duvet and sheets and pillows dumped in the corner behind the door. The wall at the head of the bed is covered in photographs, an overlapping collage.

"Take a seat, get comfortable," Joensen says. "I won't be long."

There is nowhere to sit other than the bed. She guesses this is where he wants to shoot her. She goes to it, crawls on top, stays on her knees to take a closer look at the photographs. The subjects are all women, most of them either half-dressed or naked. It doesn't look like they've been taken in the room, on the bed. It doesn't look like the women knew they were being photographed. The shots have been taken through windows. If she looks close enough she can see the reflection of light on glass. In some of the pictures there is the chipped wood of a sill visible.

The entire wall is covered, from base to ceiling, and there are a few stuck to walls to her left and right, just beginning to spread out, a crude kind of wallpaper. As she looks toward the top, she sees something out the corner of her eye, on the ceiling. There is another photograph there. Another woman. She looks into the camera with the saddest eyes Sally has ever seen.

"You like them?"

Sally turns. "Is this why I'm here?"

"No. That's my private collection."

"Did you pay them, too?"

Joensen laughs. "They don't even know."

"You peeped on them?"

He shrugs one shoulder, studies the camera in his hands.

"Is there...am I up here?"

"Could be."

She scans. "I don't see myself."

"Maybe you're not. Maybe you're under the bed. Maybe I took pictures of you but just didn't get one I liked."

She turns, sits cross-legged. "What if that happens now?"

"That's not gonna happen now."

"You're so sure?"

"This is for a specific market."

"A market?"

"Yeah."

"What're you gonna do with these pictures, if they're not goin on this wall here?"

"They're going in a magazine. A real glossy one, too. You're gonna be famous Sally, how's that feel?"

"What do you mean?"

"There's a market for everything, that's what I mean. There's even a market for pictures of young ladies such as yourself doing what you do."

"That's why I'm here?"

"That's why you're here."

"Who wants to look at that?"

"There's all kinds in this world, Sally. That's what keeps it spinning."

She draws her knees up to her chest, wraps her arms around them.

Joensen puts the camera on top of a chest of drawers pressed against the wall opposite the bed. He slides one of the drawers open and pulls out a package. He takes it to the bed, hands it over. "Once you start cooking, I'll start taking pictures."

Sally takes the package from him, licks her lips. The tip of her tongue probes the scab.

"Are you ready?"

"Yeah."

"Just do what you do. You don't even have to look at me. This ain't a fashion shoot, I don't want you to make love to the camera. The folks that are gonna look at these pictures, they don't care about any of that shit. If I give you instructions, and you can still hear them, then just do as I say. This'll be the easiest money you'll ever make."

Sally lowers her legs into a crossed position, opens the package and spreads it out. Inside is everything she needs for a hit. She tries not to think about her nudity, about Joensen stood nearby with his camera. She has done worse for a hit.

The needle and the tourniquet, the small foil wrapper filled with heroin, they all help to clear her mind, to take away the self-awareness, to dull her to her situation, where she is, what is happening.

She unwraps the foil, pours the powder into the spoon. Already, Joensen has started taking pictures. She can hear the click of the camera. She ignores it. The flame from the lighter is strong, the cartridge full with gas, unused.

The powder begins to cook, to bubble. When it is ready, she soaks it up with cotton wool. The pack is well-equipped, the works better prepared and organised than her own. The needle is certainly cleaner. She wonders how many shoots like this he has done, how long it has taken to amass such equipment, and to gain an apparent knowledge of how to prepare and use it.

She presses the needlepoint to the wool, draws out the plunger, fills the syringe, then takes the rubber tubing tourniquet and wraps it round the top of her left bicep. She taps the inside of her elbow until a thin vein appears. She pushes the tip of the needle into her skin, draws out a little blood with the plunger, then pumps it in.

"Look at me," Joensen says.

She raises her eyes. He snaps a picture of her face.

It begins to take hold. She closes her eyes, begins to sway. "I'm gonna lie down."

"Do whatever you want, Sally."

She lies back, feels herself sink into the mattress like she is floating on a cloud. She looks up to the ceiling, to the sad-eyed girl looking back at her.

The corners of her vision are soft, unfocussed, like she is in a television dream. It feels like she is smiling, a smile that will stay on her face forever. Everything has gone – life, the day-to-day, the pain of her scabs and the pain in her belly, the taste of vomit and blood – everything is peace.

The room goes dark. She rides that darkness, floats on it, carried along by angels that sing sweet songs in her ears.

When she wakes it is morning. She can see weak shafts of light leaking through the gaps at the sides of the curtains and down the middle. She feels sick. Everything hurts. She is on the mattress still. There is a blanket on top of her. Her clothes are on the floor next to the bed. They have been folded.

Joensen sits at the table in the kitchen, eating brightly coloured cereal. He smiles when she enters the room. "Morning," he says.

Sally takes a seat.

"Would you like some?" He shakes the box.

"No, thank you."

"Toast?"

"I'm not hungry."

He shrugs, finishes the bowl then pours another.

Sally rubs her arms. The spot where the needle went in is itchy. She scratches it through the cardigan sleeve. Joensen concentrates on his food. He eats with his mouth open and breathes noisily. "How did it go?" Sally says. "Was I – was it…okay?"

He speaks with the spoon still in his mouth. "The shoot? It went great. You were great. I'll get finished up here then I'll get your money."

"Okay." She struggles to watch him eat. She hates the way he talks with his mouth filled, but she hates the silence, punctuated by his slobbering, more. It is better to keep him talking. "The pictures – they're good?"

"Yeah. I'm real happy with them."

"Will I ever see them?"

He grins. "I doubt that."

The bowl is half gone. A thought occurred to Sally the night before, as she pumped the heroin into her veins, and it returns to her now. "I was wondering, what'll you do if someone ever OD's on one of your shoots?"

He stops eating, looks at her for a long time. "I'd take them outside, and dump them in the alley round back."

"You'd dump them?"

"They'd know the risk coming in. You knew the risk coming in, right? You know the risk every time you stick that needle in your arm. And, no offence, but no one's gonna bat an eyelid at a dead junkie slumped behind a dumpster. It might be a shock to see, at first, but people kinda expect it to happen sooner or later."

Sally sucks in the corner of her mouth, sucks on the scab. "We're people."

"Yeah, and I'd be real heartbroken, but what the fuck else would you have me do?"

"Would you take a few pictures first, before you dumped them?"

He looks at her a little longer but says nothing, then returns to his cereal, spoons up the last few sugar-bound clusters, then raises the bowl to his mouth and drains the milk. Drops of it fall from his bottom lip, down his chin, splash onto his already food-stained t-shirt. He pushes away from the table, stands. "I'll get your money," he says.

Sally stands too, straightens out her clothes, meets him in the hallway.

He hands her fifty bucks in crumpled, greasy bills. His smile has returned. "Anyway, nice to meet you, Sally." He steers her toward the door.

She slows. "Will you need me again?"

"Maybe. Not soon. I'm looking for new models at the minute. Hey, if you know anyone that might be interested, give them my number. Just like Lucy did for you, right? We'll get some more fresh meat out there, then we'll be ready for a second go round, how's that sound?"

"How'll I know?"

He shrugs, tilts his head slightly. "Give me another call in a few months, we'll see what we can do. Think you can do that?"

"Months?"

Joensen shrugs again, opens the door for her to leave. "It is what it is. If you're interested still, call me. Hey, times change. Maybe you'll be clean by then and it'll be the last thing on your mind, huh?" He laughs, like he's made some kind of joke.

What he didn't say was, *If you're not dead.*

"Sure, okay." She steps outside. "I'll call you. I've still got your number."

"That's great, Sally." He is smiling still, showing all his beaming teeth, bits of food from the night before still stuck in them. "I'll look forward to hearing from you." He closes the door.

Sally stands there. Everything feels rushed from the moment she woke, like maybe she is dreaming. She looks down at the bills in her hand, counts them out again. She clutches them tight in one fist, then goes down the stairs and leaves the building.

    Outside, it is cold still. It looks like it's going to rain.

The Boy

1

Jake stops outside the trailer. One hand rests on the railing that leads up the steps to the door, and he listens. There are voices inside. There is laughter. His father has company. Jake hesitates, thinks about staying out longer, taking a chance on the company being gone when he returns, or their at least being passed out, but he has nowhere else to go and it is dark and cold, getting colder, so he stashes his skateboard under the trailer and goes inside.

The air is thick with cigarette smoke and beer fumes, and he can smell marijuana. Harry sits on the sofa with a dark-skinned woman in his lap. On the table before them stand half-empty bottles of beer, some almost filled to the neck with dumped cigarette butts, and between the bottles is a mess of what looks like an aborted attempt at rolling a joint. Harry looks up as his son enters, spreads out his arms. "Jacob!" he says.

Jake nods.

"Where've you been, boy?"

Jake tries not to stare at the woman, focuses on his father. "Out," he says.

Harry is a thickset man, with workman's muscles popping at the short sleeves of his shirt. His hair is thin on top, and his face is unshaven. His top lip sports a scruffy moustache. "That so? Who with?"

"Ray. And Glenn."

Harry snorts. "Those peckerheads, huh?"

Jake says nothing.

"Come sit with us!"

The woman hangs from Harry's shoulders, her arms wrapped around him, her legs draped across his lap. One long-fingered hand strokes his cheek and from where her head rests in the crook of his neck she smiles at Jake.

Jake shifts his weight from one leg to the other. He doesn't want to sit with his father, or his new friend.

"This here's Maggie," Harry says, tilting his head toward the woman beside him, her legs in his lap. "We met at the bar. Say hello to Maggie."

"Hello, Maggie."

"Hello, Jacob." She giggles. The way she sits, coupled with the shortness of her dress, means Jake can see all of her leg, from the tips of her barefoot toes to the relaxed muscle of her thigh, to the curve of her left buttock, all the way to her waist. If he looks past the left leg, to the right, he can see the inside of her thigh. He snaps his attention back to her face. Her shoulders are bare, it doesn't look like she is wearing a bra, and the top of her dress rides low, it barely covers her nipples. He concentrates on her face. It is smooth and heart-shaped and kindly and her eyes are bright and brown and round and her lips look like chocolate. "Your daddy told me about you, but he never said how handsome you is."

"That's cos he ain't."

Maggie rears back, slaps Harry on the arm. "Now don't be mean, you."

Harry waves her off, laughs. "Ah, he knows I'm just kiddin with him. That's what we do. Ain't it, boy?"

"That's what we do," Jake says. He grits his teeth and tries not to stare at Maggie, though it is hard when she keeps smiling at him with her sweet face and her mega-watt teeth.

And the way her dress rides down just a little further every time she moves, like it is too loose on her, or like the back has been unzipped.

"Come on and sit with us, damn it," Harry says. "Come take a seat."

"I think I'm gonna go to bed –"

"Bullshit! Don't be rude, boy, we got company! Come and sit down – hell, get yourself a drink if you want. And while you're over there, get me another. You want another one, Maggie?"

"I'm all right for now, sweetie."

"Get me hers, too. No point lettin it go to waste." Harry and Maggie laugh at each other, pinch and tickle each other.

Jake gets the two beers, finds a space on the table and sets them down, then parks himself in the chair opposite. The smell of the weed on the table is strong.

"Roll one up, boy," Harry says. "I'd do it myself, but I got more fingers than usual." He holds out the back of his hand, squints at it.

Jake gets to his knees, pulls the table and everything on top of it closer

173

to him, gets to work rolling.

"Woo," Maggie says. "Looks like you've done this before."

Jake says nothing.

"He's had practise," Harry says.

"For you?"

"I should reckon for no one else. Sometimes your old man sprouts a few more fingers than usual, huh, boy?"

Jake looks at Maggie. "That means he's seeing double."

Maggie laughs, Harry too. "You gettin sassy, boy?"

"No, sir."

"Aw, c'mon – that's a damn shame. For a second there I thought you might actually show a little character. Maggie, this kid, he goes to school, comes home, locks himself away in his room all damn night. I dunno *what* he's doin in there – well, I can take a coupla guesses." He nudges her with his elbow. "But when he's not sprainin his wrist, what's he doin, you tell me that."

"He said he'd been out with his friends, Harry," Maggie says. "He don't go and see his friends too much?"

Harry blows air. "Those two kids've got shit-for-brains. Bout damn time you put down that fuckin skateboard and found yourself some new friends."

Jake finishes rolling, passes the joint to his father, then returns to his seat.

Harry holds it upright, between thumb and index finger, gives a low whistle. "My, my," he says. "That is a thing of beauty, boy." He shows it to Maggie. "He does have some admirable skills though, I will give him that. And I'll tell you another thing, he's improved a damn sight – a few years back, first time I asked him to roll me one, you shoulda seen the mess he made. Wasted half the damn bud. But he's persevered, and look at him now. God damn."

Maggie looks at Jake, shoots him a secret grin, winks. Jake shifts in his seat.

"Move your legs now, girl, I'll light this thing up." Harry reaches across the table for his lighter, purses the roached end between his lips and lights it at the other. He inhales deeply, passes it to Maggie. Jake watches her. Her sleek black hair is cut short, it frames her face when she leans forward like she is, and her dress drops down a little more. Jake bites his lip, grits his teeth, looks at his hands.

Harry holds it out. "Take a hit."

"I'm all right."

"Damn it, boy, you rolled the damn thing, take a draw on it."

"If he doesn't want –" Maggie says.

Harry cuts her off. "He don't want a drink, he don't want a smoke – what does he want? He wants to go back to that room of his, that fuckin black hole. You're bein mighty rude in fronta company, boy. Take it."

Jake stares at the burning stick held before him in his father's gnarled and work-dirty fist. He takes it, presses it to his lips. It isn't his first time smoking, but he doesn't make a habit of it. It hits him hard, knocks him dizzy. He starts to cough, covers his mouth with the back of his hand and gives it to Maggie. Harry claps him on the arm so hard he almost falls out the chair.

"Good shit, ain't it?" Harry says. "You ain't had it like that before. Some fuckin good shit. Now. You want that drink yet?" His eyes are narrowed in a way that says *No* is the wrong answer.

Jake coughs. "Sure."

"Well you know where the refrigerator is," Harry says. "Grab some potato chips while you're over there."

Jake stands, sways when he is fully erect, takes deep breaths. The room spins. He looks down, feels exceptionally tall. From up high, he can see right down Maggie's dress, straight down the deep valley that separates one breast from the other.

"Hey, boy," Harry says.

Jake blinks at him.

"You might wanna tuck that thing away, too." He points.

Jake looks down. He is hard, the shape of his dick presses tight against the front of his jeans.

Maggie covers her mouth with her hand, tries not to laugh.

Jake stumbles away, adjusts himself. "I'm gonna go to bed," he says, but he mumbles it and can't be sure if anyone hears him.

"Hey, boy!" Harry says. He is laughing. "What about the potato chips!"

2

The sound of the wheels rolling fast along the tarmac is deafening. The dark road ahead clear of headlights, Jake closes his eyes and feels the wind whip his face and his hair. Behind him he hears one of the others, probably Glenn, do a jump.

He opens his eyes and skids to a stop, kicks his board up into his hands and carries it. The others do the same. They cross the road and go into the park. It is late and dark, people wearing black that don't want to be seen move like shadows upon the paths and the grass. Bushes shake. There are moans. In the distance, someone is throwing up.

They near the water feature in the centre of the park, the graffiti-decorated cherub pouring water. A man reclines on one of the benches. He wears a cowboy hat and smokes a cigarette, the tip glows incredibly bright. They go to him.

"Fellas," he says, nods. "Where y'all off to?"

Ray approaches the man. Ray is the tallest of them, he always does the talking. "Will you buy us beer?"

The cowboy uncrosses his legs, leans forward. "What's in it for me?"

"We'll give you a bottle."

"Two."

"Sure."

He stubs out his cigarette against the bench then deposits the butt in his chest pocket. "Where you plannin on drinkin them?"

"What?"

"The beers. Where you gonna drink them?"

Ray looks back then shrugs. "I dunno."

"Here? In the park?"

"I dunno. Maybe."

The cowboy clasps his hands, looks each of them over while he talks. "Now, I suspect the three of you are the kind of good boys that would take your trash away with you, right? Dispose of those bottles responsibly?"

"What?"

"We don't need anymore litter round here, you get me?"

Ray turns, shakes his head. "Whatever, man." They walk.

"Hey – I said I'd get your beer."

They ignore him, continue through the park, pass a woman in a witch's Halloween mask where she leans against a railing. She focuses on Jake. He looks back. He can't see her eyes, but he can feel them. She watches him pass, her head moving with him. She breathes heavily, then when he is past and still looking back at her she begins a rasping giggle.

When they exit the other end of the park, the liquor store is in sight.

"What're we gonna do?" Glenn says.

"Just wait," Ray says. "Someone will show up."

The liquor store has a neon sign in the window flashing OPEN in red, and beyond that they can see the light inside, the bored clerk behind the counter.

"He might just serve us," Glenn says.

"No," Jake says. "Look at him. He's bored as fuck. Turning us down would be the highlight of his night. It'd be a power trip for him."

Ray nods along, snorts. "Probably the only kind of power he's got."

"It'll get him off."

"Yeah. He looks like a prick. If we go in now and he turns us away it'll just tip him off. He'll be ultra cautious of everyone else."

The clerk is a young guy, probably just turned old enough to drink himself. His hair is dark and his fringe is long, hangs down into his face so he keeps blowing it out of his glasses. He stares at the counter, probably reading a magazine.

"Let's get closer," Glenn says. "So we can catch someone going in."

As they cross the road, a man goes inside.

"Shit," Glenn says. "We've missed him."

The man's hood is pulled up. When they get outside the store they see that he has a gun, that he is waving it in the clerk's face. The clerk is deathly pale, his lips are moving, like he's babbling, he looks like he's trying not to shit himself. He opens the cash register, lets the gunman help himself.

"Holy fuck," Ray says.

They watch through the window.

The money bagged, the man waves the gun in the clerk's face again. The clerk flinches, begs off. The gunman grabs him by the shirtfront, drags him over the counter, beats him with the gun's handle. The clerk's cheek splits, he spits blood and teeth, his glasses smash and his left eye swells up. The gunman kicks him for good measure then turns and runs, blows past the three of them and disappears down the street. Jake watches him go. He expects to hear sirens, but he doesn't. Behind him, the door to the liquor store opens again. He turns and sees that Glenn has run inside.

"What's he doing?"

Ray laughs. Glenn has pulled his hat down so most of his face is obscured from the camera. He grabs a crate and a couple of loose bottles then bolts out of the store and keeps running and Ray and Jake run after him and Ray is still laughing.

3

It is night. Cold. Jake's breath mists. He wears black, keeps his hands in his pockets and walks casually, no hurry, like he's on his way to meet friends, or is out for the air, but as he nears his destination he begins to slow. He checks the windows of the nearby trailers, ensures that curtains are closed and blinds are drawn, that no one lurks in the darkness. When he is sure there is not, that no one is looking, he drops to a stoop, begins to creep.

He presses his body against Luann's trailer, stands on his toes until he's tall enough he can see through the gap between the bottom of the curtain and the window frame. The outside of the trailer feels cool against his mouth and nose.

The inside is well-lit. Luann is there, alone, her parents out somewhere, probably a bar. She is in the kitchen. She opens the refrigerator, pulls out orange juice, drinks it straight from the carton. She looks like she is about to go to bed, wears a white vest and black underwear. Her dark hair is piled atop her head, and under her vest she wears no bra. The cold from the refrigerator makes her nipples hard, two sharp points probe outwards from the small mounds of her breasts. Jake stares at her chest, feels his breath misting against the side of the trailer, it tickles his nostrils. Her legs are long and toned, the right is bent slightly and the left straight while she stands and drinks.

She puts the carton back, closes the refrigerator. She steps barefoot across the floor, takes a seat on the sofa, draws her legs under herself, and flicks on the television. Jake watches her, watches the side of her face. She plays with the remote control, spins it slowly round in her hands. Her eyes narrow then and she turns toward him. He ducks, keeps his head below the window for a count of twenty, then slowly straightens up. She has turned back to the television.

An engine approaches from the front. Luann looks up, bites her lip. She pulls the band out of her hair and shakes it loose so it is wild and curly like she hasn't long gotten out the shower and it is still wet.

Jake ducks from the window, creeps to the side of the trailer, peers round as the truck comes to a stop and the engine and lights are switched off. He knows the truck. Knows the guy that gets out, makes his way up the porch steps to knock on the trailer's door. Ricky. He is older than Jake, older than Luann. Maybe eighteen. Maybe twenty-one. He is tall and broad, wears jeans and a leather jacket, looks like he plays sports. The door opens. Jake goes back to the window.

He can see Luann at the door, sees the way her underwear clings to the curves of her buttocks. Sees the way she sways slightly from side to side, coquettishly plays with her hair. She hasn't let Ricky in yet. Jake can't hear what they are saying, but he can hear her laugh. And then she lets him in.

They stand in the kitchen. Luann plays with the zip on Ricky's jacket.

They are very close to each other. Ricky smiles down at Luann. He looks cool, composed, but Jake can see the hunger in his eyes, can sense it coming off him in waves, even from outside.

They kiss. Luann turns her face up and stands on her toes. Ricky's hands go round her waist, settle in the dip of her lower back. She seems incredibly small against him, about a foot shorter and half his width.

They go to the sofa, mouths locked. Luann takes off her vest, but her back is to Jake and he can't see anything good, just the ridges of her spine. Ricky takes off his clothes. Starts with his jacket, then his t-shirt. Luann helps him. His torso ripples with muscle, smooth and hairless, his nipples small and dark. Luann presses her mouth to them, kisses them each in turn.

They stand then. Luann slips off her underwear. Jake can see the crack of her ass. She gets Ricky out of his jeans, undoes his belt buckle and his buttons like he is incapable. He lifts her up suddenly, kisses her neck. Jake can hear her squeal. Ricky lies her down on the sofa. His dick looks so hard it must have been crushed inside his jeans. The slit at the tip of it looks straight at Jake like an angry eye, spots him where he hides, sees him, knows him, threatens to tell the whole room what he is doing.

"*Hey.*"

Jake's breath catches. He spins, sees a figure step out of the gloom.

"What're you doin, kid?"

Jake panics, turns to run, his right foot trips over his left ankle and he falls, sprawls flat on his face in the dirt, tastes it gritty in his teeth. He tries to push up, tells himself he can still get away, but the shadowy figure is on him, has him by the collar. A clamp-like grip, incredibly strong, hauls him to his feet. Jake tries to struggle.

"Get off me!" he says. He snarls it. "I ain't doin anythin wrong!"

The shadow gives him a shake. "That so?" The voice is a drawl. Jake can smell whiskey on the man's breath. His face is rough and cavernous, its wrinkles and edges deepened by the shadows. Jake thinks he recognises him, maybe one of his father's old work buddies, it is hard to tell. They all look the same, skin leathery from years of working outdoors in the weather, and nights spent drinking hard and smoking heavily.

Still holding him, the man goes to Luann's trailer, lifts his head a little to see through the gap where Jake was watching. He grunts, then the noise turns into a chuckle, and he looks back at Jake. "Weren't doin anythin wrong, huh?"

"I ain't hurtin anybody."

"That's a fact. Sayin that, I don't reckon the two of them would be too pleased if they knew you were out here watchin them." He pauses, tilts his head. "Then again, I don't reckon the girl's parents know she's entertainin." The man pulls him closer, leans him into light that shines weakly from a security lamp three trailers down. "Ain't you Harry's boy?"

Jake goes limp. He's been made. "Yes, sir."

"You don't remember me, huh?" The man's grip, though his hands stay in place, goes loose.

"You look familiar."

"Well, it's been a long time since I saw you last, too. Few years at the least. I'm Carlson."

The name sounds familiar. "Okay." He doesn't know what else to say.

"I used to work with your daddy, back when the mill was operatin. Where's he now – still at the bottle factory?"

"Yeah."

Carlson lets go of Jake but stays close, looks like he is thinking. "You do this kind of thing regular?"

"How do you mean?"

"Peepin – watchin folk."

Jake lies. "No sir."

Carlson studies him with one eye. "Tell you what – this one time, I'll let you off. You get outta here, and we'll pretend we never talked. But I catch you again, I'll drag you to your daddy, y'understand?"

Jake nods. "Yessir."

"Good." Carlson sounds satisfied. "Get outta here, then."

Jake turns, runs into the dark, takes care not to trip over his feet again. He slows when he is far enough away, stops and looks back. Carlson stands where Jake had been, he peers through the gap, watches them inside the trailer, watches Luann. His hand is in his pocket, and it is not still.

Jake feels hot tears sting his eyes, tears of shame and frustration at getting caught. Even thoughts of Luann, what little he had seen, aren't enough to shake the darkness from his mind. He shoves his hands deep in his pockets, grits his teeth, and takes a slow walk home.

4

Jake sleeps late, wakes to the sound of the toilet flushing. He lies on his stomach, rolls onto his back and sits up on the edge of the bed, runs his hands back through his hair and sees he is still dressed in the clothes of the night before. He yawns, stretches, hears his stomach grumble, but he doesn't move. He sits still, listens. Whoever flushed the toilet, either Maggie or his father, is in there still. The shower is turned on, the door slides open, then closed again, then the water pounds against the walls and the occupant's body.

Jake's room is small, cramped, barely big enough to accommodate his single bed. Where he sits, his knees touch the wall which separates his room from the bathroom. On the mornings when his father is in there throwing up the over-indulgence of the night before, the sound is thunderous and echoes through the thin walls. The flushing of the toilet, the running of the taps or shower, aren't quite so extreme.

At the base of the bed is a narrow wardrobe, sat atop crates so its doors clear the mattress when they are opened. On the floor next to his headboard is a small stack of comic books. He has a few band posters on his walls, an attempt to give the room some personality, but there is not much space and they all overlap.

Jake peers out the door. The sitting area is a mess, but there is no one there. He goes to the kitchen, grabs a bowl and a box of cereal, pours out some milk, is on his way back to his room when his father's door opens. Harry steps out from the gloom, yawns and scratches the back of his head. He wears his underwear and a sweat-stained vest, his pale arms and legs on show. The shower is still running – Maggie. She has been in the trailer for a few days now. Jake doesn't know when she left to get more of her stuff, but she seems to have made herself at home. Her washed clothes hang from the windows, she has a toothbrush in the bathroom, and she has brought her own towels.

Harry smoothes out his moustache with the flat of his hand, narrows his eyes. "What time's it?"

"I don't know."

Harry shuffles to the kitchen, prises open the blinds and looks outside, winces as daylight greets him. "How come you ain't at school?"

"It's summer vacation."

"It is?"

"Yeah."

"Since when?"

"A week ago."

"Shit, boy, you don't tell me nothin." He nods at the bowl in Jake's hands. "You not gonna make your old man somethin?"

Jake holds back a sigh. "What do you want?"

"We got eggs?"

"I don't know."

Harry checks. "We've got eggs. I'll have eggs. You know how I like em."

"What about Maggie?"

"What about her?"

"Will she want any?"

"I dunno, ask her yourself." He grins then, a twinkle in his eye like he's remembered something. "You like Maggie?"

"She's okay."

Harry's grin broadens. "Wait until she gets outta the shower before you ask her though."

Harry steps past him, still smiling, sits at the coffee table where bagged drugs lie, and the paraphernalia to accompany them. He looks at his hands, checks the amount of fingers there, then starts to roll. While he does, he picks up a bottle with some beer left in the bottom and drinks it down.

Jake stays in the kitchen, leans against the bench and eats his cereal. Harry has left the door to his bedroom open and there is a familiar stench leaking out of sweat-filtered alcohol.

The shower stops running. Jake feels his breath catch. He shovels more cereal into his mouth and chews hard, stares into the bowl. The shower door slides open, then closes again. Jake spoons in more cereal.

The bathroom door opens. Over the top of his bowl Jake spies the bottom of Maggie's legs, streaked with rivulets of water, as her bare feet step out onto the carpet. "Hello, Jake," she says. He has to look.

She beams at him, shows off all her perfect white teeth. Her hair is slicked back from her forehead, tucked behind her ears. A blue towel is wrapped around her, covers her. Water glistens on her shoulders and the top of her chest.

Jake realises he hasn't said anything. "Uh, hi," he says, mumbles, barely audible. Maggie keeps smiling.

"Jacob's about to make eggs," Harry says. He is leaning back into the corner of the sofa, speaks like he is holding his breath, the freshly rolled joint burning in his hand. "Want some?"

"How you makin them?"

The bowl is empty now but Jake clings to it, like it is some kind of shield to hide behind, like it can hide anything he is feeling and the evidence of anything that might be happening below the waist. "Scrambled."

"Sounds good," she says, then disappears into the bedroom, closes the door. Jake lets out a breath then, shaky and ragged like he's been holding it in a long time. Harry watches him. He chuckles.

Jake turns away quickly, gets to work with the eggs, cracks them into a bowl and mixes them up. He pours the mixture into a frying pan then looks at his father. He holds up the joint. Jake scratches behind his ear, says nothing.

"You interested?"

Jake changes the subject. "You're not at work today?"

Harry lowers the joint. "Nope. Week off."

"You don't tell me nothin," Jake says.

Harry laughs.

Maggie returns, dressed but still towelling her hair. "What's so funny?" she says.

"Ah, nothin," Harry says. "Smoke?"

Maggie joins him. "Don't mind if I do." She wears tight jeans and a loose shirt. Jake waits for the day she wears the dress again, the dress she wore the first night he saw her, riding low on her breasts and with her ass almost hanging out. Every morning she emerges from the room wearing something different he feels a surge of disappointment.

"So," Harry says, and it is clear from the way his voice is raised that he is talking to Jake, calling across the room. "Since there's no school, what've you got planned for the day?"

Jake takes the pan off the heat, spoons the eggs onto plates. "I'm goin out," he says.

"You don't wanna spend some quality time with your old man?"

"Sorry."

"Where you goin?"

"I dunno. Just out."

"With who?"

"Friends."

Harry roars laughter.

"Jesus Christ, Harry," Maggie says. "Not so loud – you scared the crap outta me there, right in my damn ear."

"I'm sorry, honey. It's just the three fuckin musketeers over there. Y'know, those two boys won't set foot on the trailer park. Scared. Think we're all a bunch a inbred cannibals or somethin."

Jake takes them the eggs, sets both plates down on the table along with the bottle of tomato ketchup he's carried over tucked in his armpit. His father has a specific ratio to how he likes his plate: two-thirds egg to one-third ketchup.

"I'm sure that ain't what they think," Maggie says.

"They're town folk, honey," Harry says, puts an arm round her shoulder and pulls her close to him. "That's what they all think." He puts his mouth close to her ear, speaks low so Jake isn't supposed to hear, but Jake hears. "There's only one part of a person I'm willin to eat, and they gotta be a female at that."

Maggie hits him on the arm, but she giggles. She looks up, meets Jake's eye. Jake looks away, busies himself in the kitchen.

Harry squeezes half the bottle of ketchup onto his plate. "Come over here and sit with us a spell, boy. You in a rush?"

Jake grabs his jacket. He tries not to look at Maggie, tries to focus solely on his father. "Sorry," he says. "I'm in a rush."

5

Jake sits in a booth at the back of a diner with Ray. Glenn is in the toilet, through the door that advertises men with a framed black and white photograph of an old movie star that Jake doesn't recognise. They share a bowl of onion rings that swim in grease, and another bowl of fries that are lukewarm and stiff. Ray doesn't seem to mind. He shovels handfuls of each into his mouth, chews quickly and swallows as if he is trying to finish them off before Glenn can return. Jake chews idly on an onion ring, holds it at the corner of his mouth with his left hand while his right traces the outline of the letters JC carved into the table.

A few booths down sit a group of girls they go to school with. The girls talk loudly but it is hard to tell what they are saying, a barrage of garbled noise that assaults the ears. An old man sits alone at a table across from them and he grimaces at their speech, probably just wants to eat his cremated burger in peace. One of the girls writes on the wall between the windows with a felt marker pen, on a space between all the license plates and cartoons. The waitress doesn't seem to care, too preoccupied flirting with the bartender, her back to the room.

Glenn leaves the toilet, sees the girls, makes eye contact with one of them and lowers his head, hurries back to the booth, sits so they are behind him. "When did they get here?" he says.

"Not too long ago," Ray says.

Glenn slaps his hand. "Slow down – Jesus Christ."

Ray looks past him. A couple of the girls look over, talk amongst themselves, one of them laughs loudly. "What's the deal?"

Glenn shakes his head. "You see the girl with the braces?"

Ray and Jake look. She sees them and turns away quickly, hides her face behind a menu. "Uh-huh."

"I've been with her."

Jake raises an eyebrow.

"Oh yeah?"

"Yeah. I mean, we didn't fuck. But we made out. She let me put a finger in."

"When was this?"

"Coupla months back. Her parents are friendly with my parents, it was at her mom's birthday party, her fiftieth or somethin. They were lettin us drink."

"She musta gotten pretty drunk," Ray says.

"Fuck you." Glenn picks absently at the remnant of a scab on his chin from where he took a fall from his skateboard a few weeks back. "She took me up to her room."

"Did she seduce you?" Ray grins.

"Shit, I dunno. Maybe she did."

"How come it didn't go any further?"

"I fell asleep."

Ray laughs. "What did she do?"

"I don't know. I woke up alone. She must've told everyone I'd put myself to bed, because no one seemed to care that I was in her room."

Jake glances at their table. The girl with the braces keeps stealing looks, all of them do.

"What's she doing? Is she looking?"

"Yes."

"Aw, let's just get out of here."

Ray picks up a fry, suddenly taking his time. "Hey – we're still eating." He smiles as he chews, lumps of potato between the gaps in his teeth.

Jake looks out the window to their left. Movement catches his eye. A woman passes, holds the hand of a little girl. The woman has dark hair, cut short. Sports a grey t-shirt and faded jeans, she isn't wearing make-up. She is Jake's mother. The girl is his half-sister, her father is his mother's new husband. He has never met the husband, or his sister, or the other child not present, the boy, his brother. He watches them pass, disappear from view. He feels the familiar hot angry knot balling in his stomach. He grits his teeth and turns away from the window.

He doesn't feel the gnawing ebb of abandonment anymore, like he used. It has been a long time since he last felt that longing. What he feels now is more akin to hate.

Ray and Glenn are still talking about the girl. He can't hear them. He bites his lip and looks round the diner. The old man has finished, he is leaving. The waitress still talks to the bartender, doesn't notice the old man leave. The girl with the braces meets his eye. They look at each other for a moment.

"Let's go," Jake says.

"I'm still eating," Ray says.

Jake stands. Glenn joins him.

Ray blows air. "Whatever," he says. He shovels in a few more fries, another onion ring, follows them as they leave.

A couple of the girls call out in a sing-song voice as they pass. "*Hi, Glenn.*"

Glenn pauses, nods. "Ladies," he says.

"Where you off to in such a rush?"

"Don't you want to sit with us?"

Jake recognises the girls, but he does not know any of them by name. They are in different classes to he, some of them are older.

Glenn, despite his earlier cowering, is unfazed. "Sorry, ladies, but we've got somewhere to be."

"Come on, Glenn – come take a nap with us."

The girl with the braces says nothing, stares intently at the tabletop and turns a painful shade of red.

Glenn cocks his head to one side, holds out his arms. "Sorry, but I'm good. I've already had my nap today. Shame, right? But what you gonna do?" He sniffs the index and middle fingers of his right hand, runs them slowly under his nose, and the girls let out a noise like *Ooooooo!* or maybe *Ewwwww*! and Glenn laughs and says, "Catch y'all later!"

The three of them leave. The waitress doesn't turn. She flicks her hair and laughs at something the bartender says.

They ride their skateboards down the street to an old warehouse, empty for years, most of the windows smashed, they go round the back and practise jumps in what used to be the loading area. Jake thinks about his mother.

6

The trailer's walls are thin.

Jake can hear them, through the bathroom next door, he can hear them in his father's bedroom, he can hear what they are doing to each other. Can hear his father's laboured grunting, and Maggie's lighter gasps. He can feel it, too, the way the trailer rocks with their thrusting.

They say things, between all the panting. Dirty-talk. Their voices are muffled. He can't make it out.

Jake crawls out of bed, gets dressed and creeps from his room, goes outside, closes the door and sits on the step in the cool night air. He can still hear them. Maggie's cries get louder, until she unleashes an orgasmic squeal. His father begins to laugh, but it is not over. They don't stop. He can hear the banging still.

He walks, walks fast until he is away from the trailer, from the noise, until he can't hear them anymore. Maggie occupies his mind, and he tries to hold onto her but thoughts of his father intrude. Her heavy breathing resounds in his ears, and he quietly imitates it.

After a while he takes a seat, parks himself on the steps of another trailer. He looks up, cranes his neck to see the stars, the thousands and thousands of them twinkling there in the clear sky. In the distance, something howls – a dog, or a wolf. He ignores it, too far away to be of any concern.

The moon is full. Its silvery rays shine down and give the dark objects that surround him – the trailers and parked cars; the drying clothes hanging from lines; bicycles dumped in overgrown grass – an eerie glow.

The stars, the moon, hold him for a long time. He looks at them until it feels like he's not on Earth anymore, like he's up there with them, floating through them, the world doesn't exist, it's been swallowed up by light, and he's part of the stars, the universe, the eternal everything and nothing.

A door opens opposite. Footsteps on a wooden porch. Jake looks. An old woman steps closer to her wooden railing. She is naked. Her mottled flesh hangs loose and her breasts sag down almost to her waist, one resting on either side of her bulging, stretch-marked stomach. She, too, glows in the moonlight.

"Hi," she says. There are maybe three teeth in her mouth. She cocks one hip and puts a hand on it, rests her other hand on the railing, posing. "Cold out."

Jake can see the dead veins in her legs black under her otherwise bright white skin. He stands up and walks away.

"Where're you goin, lover? What's the rush?"

Jake doesn't look back. Eventually, she stops calling him, or else he is too far away to hear her.

He turns left and realises he is at Luann's trailer, as if his feet have unconsciously carried him here. It is a moment before he realises Luann is outside, sitting on her steps, smoking a cigarette. She looks up as he rounds the corner. Jake feels himself slow.

"Hey," she says.

He nods. "Hello."

She inhales, the tip burns brightly. Her face, like everything else, is palely lit by the moonlight. "Out for a midnight stroll?"

Jake scratches the back of his neck. "Guess so."

She looks him over, quietly appraises him while she smokes. "I know you."

Jake doesn't know what to say so he shrugs.

"We go to the same school, right?"

"Uh, yeah – yeah, I think we do."

"You look familiar."

"Yeah, you too."

Jake steps closer, intent to remain engaged in conversation with her.

"Do you want a cigarette?"

"Sure."

She hands him one. He purses it between his lips and lights it from the tip of hers. Their faces are close, their foreheads almost touch.

"Thanks."

"No problem."

Jake stifles a cough then blows smoke rings, hoping to impress her, but she doesn't notice. She's not looking. "Nice night," he says.

"Yeah, it's real clear, ain't it."

"Lot of stars."

She looks up as if she hadn't noticed. "To be honest, I just want to go to bed."

"Oh." He's not sure if that is a hint for him to go. "What's stopping you?"

"My parents snore. They snore really fucking loud."

She's grinning, so Jake grins too. He is surprised that her parents are home, but he talks to her as if he knows nothing about her, or them. "So...what? They keep you awake every night?"

She shakes her head. "Most nights they go out. I'm asleep before they get back. Tonight they surprised me. Tonight they came back early, they beat me to bed." She shrugs. "They drink a lot, and – I dunno. Maybe that's what makes it so loud, you think?"

"Could be. My dad drinks a lot, and he snores pretty loud when he's passed out on the sofa."

"Then you know what I'm talkin about. He snoring right now, that why you're out here?"

"Yeah, somethin like that."

"What's your name?"

"It's Jake."

"Jake." She repeats it, tries it out. "I'm Luann."

"Luann." He repeats it as if he's hearing it, saying it, for the very first time.

"Smoking buddy," she says.

He smiles. "That's me."

"Don't you usually hang out with those two guys –" She clicks her fingers, remembering. "– one of them's really tall, got real bad acne. I don't know their names. The other one never takes off his fuckin beanie."

"Ray and Glenn. Ray's the tall one."

"Yeah, yeah – I can picture you now. Skater boys?"

"We skate."

"Ah, but that doesn't define your existence, right?"

"What?"

She laughs. "Nothin. I'm just messin with you."

"Oh. Right."

Luann opens her mouth then stops, looks to the right. She grins. Jake looks. A dark shape stumbles through the distant gloom, sticking to the shadows of the trailers where the light of the moon cannot touch it. The shape trips and falls, mumbles a curse, crawls back to its feet using a nearby truck, then continues on its way, gets closer.

"I think he's drunk," Luann says.

"Yeah."

The man finally steps into the light, gets close enough to see. He wears black, head to toe. The skin of his face is pulled tight, his features almost skeletal, his eyes hidden in two black pools under his brow. The man sees them, halts, gives a start. His head turns from Luann to Jake, looks at them each in turn. "You scared me," he says.

Luann shrugs one shoulder. "Sorry."

"What're you doin out here at this time?"

"Sittin. Smokin."

"You scared me," he repeats.

"We didn't know you were going to come along."

"Sittin there like a coupla fuckin ghouls."

"Ghosts."

"Huh?"

"Maybe we're ghosts."

"What?"

"Maybe you're a ghost."

"Girl, stop talkin trash. The two of you oughta get yourselves inside, get to bed. It's damn late out."

"That's so, but all I know is, I wouldn't wanna piss off a couple of ghosts, just sat mindin their own business. I'd be awful concerned they'd maybe follow me home and give me trouble for bein so fuckin rude."

The man says nothing, his thin lips pinched tight, then he continues on his way without another word. Luann turns to Jake, laughs. "Are you in a rush to get home?"

"No," he says, maybe too fast.

"Why don't you take a seat? We'll have another cigarette. I've got plenty."

7

Jake doesn't ride his skateboard. It is too loud. He walks briskly through the night, leaves the trailer park and goes into town, goes to the street where his mother lives.

She left Harry when Jake was six. She left him, too. She left him behind. He kept waiting for her to come back, to take him with her, but she never did.

She never came back.

She left him behind.

With Harry.

She lives in a house now, not a trailer. It's a big house. In the back yard there is a trampoline. Jake doesn't know what her husband does for a living, but he wears a suit.

Jake stands at the bottom of their driveway. The windows at the front of the house are all dark. He looks round and grabs a stone from the road, uses it to scratch the doors on the driver's side of the parked car. He writes BITCH on her bonnet. He throws the stone at the car so it dents a back panel, then he spits on the sidewalk and he leaves.

8

The television is on. It airs a game show. A single man competes against a married couple. If he wins, he takes the wife on three dates, during which time she has no contact with her husband. If the couple are victorious they get an all-expenses trip to the capital. It is a general knowledge quiz. Jake has seen the show a couple of times before. Sometimes single women come on, and they can win the husband. Sometimes the singleton is a homosexual.

The singles are outcasts. They always are. Too thin, too fat, too tall, too small, geeky and bookish, misshapen and malformed. The man tonight is thin and balding, wears black rimmed glasses with lenses as thick as the bottoms of milk jugs. Dwarfed by the too-large suit he's worn for the taping, he is sweating profusely and keeps wiping his mouth with the back of his hand. His voice is a nasal whine. He sniffs a lot. He isn't very smart, either. The married couple, some Ken and Barbie doppelgangers, are winning easily and you can see they know they are going to leave the studio and head straight to the airport, can see it in their laid-back, smug smiles.

It is called 'Indecent Proposals'. Jake does not think he will watch much more of it. He is passing time while his father and Maggie prepare to go out. Maggie is already dressed. She wears the outfit from the night Jake first met her. Fresh on, it is a better fit. It covers her breasts and goes down to her knees. Jake feels his eyes still drawn to it, though, especially when her back is turned and the fabric is pulled tight across her ass.

Whenever she turns he stares hard at the television screen, at the ageing host that was once upon a time a comedian, though Jake has never heard of him. If Maggie knows he is looking she doesn't seem to mind. She just smiles.

"Your daddy'll be ready soon," she says. "Then we'll be out your hair."

Jake nods. "Okay."

"Got anything planned?"

Jake shakes his head. "No."

Maggie pulls on her heels, and Jake feels like he should try to make conversation, offer something more than a monosyllabic grunt. "Where you going?"

"Just to the bar. Nowhere fancy."

"Okay. Is that where the two of you met?"

Maggie smiles. "I was sittin with a coupla girlfriends, and your daddy slides right up next to me and says 'How d'you do?' Didn't care my friends were there, he wasn't goin anywhere. You know how he can be."

"Sure."

Harry exits the bedroom, brings with him an overwhelming stink of cologne liberally applied. Jake turns up his nose but Maggie doesn't seem to mind. "Right, we're out of here. What're your plans for this fine evenin?"

"I don't have any."

Harry nods at the television. "You gonna watch that shit all night?"

"No."

"Good. But no parties either, y'hear?" His face splits into a grin.

"Okay."

"You need to lighten up, boy."

"Okay."

Harry pulls on his boots. "Hell, have a damn party, if you can drag enough people in." He wears jeans and a shirt with the top three buttons undone and too much chest hair showing. "Don't wait up." He winks.

Maggie pauses in the door on her way out. "Goodnight, Jacob." She wriggles her fingers in a wave, and then they're gone.

Jake stands, goes to the window, watches them walk away. They link arms. When they are out of sight he turns off the television. The singleton was wiping under his eyes with one finger, trying to pretend the moisture there is sweat. Jake goes to his father's room.

The bed is made, and though the air is still thick with cologne under that it does not smell like it used to of stale sweat and beer belches. He notices the window is open to let in fresh air.

Maggie is not living out of a suitcase. Her clothes have been put away. He hunts through the wardrobe and in drawers, sees that she has been designated her own section for her garments. He finds her underwear. He thinks about her in the dress, closes his eyes and remembers the way her breasts spilled from it that first night. He takes a pair of her underwear, turquoise with a little bow on the front, balls it up in his fist and goes to the bathroom, presses it to his nose and mouth and breathes it in while he masturbates.

9

The closest Ray and Glenn will get to the trailer park is the woods.

They find a clearing and sit on dead logs, gather round the remnants of a long-dead fire, dried grass and twigs scorched black. Jake thinks about Maggie, about her dress and her underwear. He thinks about Luann, about the taste of her cigarettes.

"I went to see Kelly, after the other day –" Glenn begins.

Ray interrupts. "Who?"

"Kelly – from the diner."

"Brace-face?"

Glenn grimaces. "She wears a brace, yes, if that's what you mean. Anyway, I went to see her."

"Where at?"

"Her place. I called her first, I mean I didn't just turn up. I'm not a fuckin stalker, y'know?"

Ray rolls his eyes. "Sure."

Glenn hits him on the arm. "You gonna let me tell this fuckin story, or what?"

"What happened – did she suck your dick?"

Glen's eyes gleam.

"Fuck off – no she didn't."

"No, she didn't, you're right. I wouldn't let her – those braces? She'd cut the poor guy to shreds. She gave me a handjob."

"Bull*shit*."

"Hey, you don't have to believe me. Doesn't mean it didn't happen."

Jake runs one hand back through his hair, looks through the trees and bushes. He can hear birds above. A figure moves between tree trunks. He thinks it is a man, dressed in furs and sporting wild hair, a long beard. He peers at them from around bark, but he does not come any closer. Jake does not alert the others to his presence.

"We went for a walk, and she started giving me all this soppy shit about how she thought I was really crude in the diner and that hurt her feelings because she thought we had something special and she'd been trying to talk to me since her parents' party and yadda-yadda-yadda, but basically she wants to do the whole boyfriend-girlfriend thing."

"And she grabbed your dick to prove that."

"Pretty much."

"You're full of it."

Glenn holds out his hands. "You'll see. If I'm lyin I'm dyin. The whole thing's gonna be pretty official soon."

"So she's your girlfriend."

"Yeah."

"Okay. Jake, you hearing this?"

The man in the trees is gone.

"Jake?"

"What?"

They both look at him. "What're you lookin at?" Glenn says.

Jake shrugs. "Nothing. Just thinking. We used to come here a lot more when we were kids."

"Kinda changing the subject there, Jake," Glenn says

"I'm just thinking out loud."

Ray nods. "We used to play fight, remember that? We'd jump outta the trees onto each other."

Glenn points at Ray. "You were a rough motherfucker. You would chase us with the biggest fuckin stick you could find. You bust my mouth up a couple times."

"Must be why you've got such a pretty smile."

"I remember when we found the bird," Jake says.

They look at him.

"I don't know what kind of bird it was. It was a long time ago, we were maybe eight, I can't remember. But it was brown. It wasn't big and it wasn't small. Glenn spotted it first. It was trying to fly but it couldn't. One of its wings was all busted up. It would flap really hard with its good wing but it would only get a few inches off the ground, then it would start cawing like it was shouting at itself."

Neither of them say anything.

"You tried to pick it up." He talks to Ray. "But it pecked you, and that made you mad so you threw it down, then when it was dazed you picked it back up, and you tore it apart. You grabbed each wing, and you pulled until it burst."

Ray speaks quietly. "That didn't happen."

"It did. I remember it. I think about it every time I come into the woods. You dropped it, but it wasn't dead. So you stepped on its head, and Glenn said it was a mercy killing." He turns to Glenn. "Then you dipped your fingers in its blood, and you put the blood on your cheeks, like warpaint. Then you painted Ray's face with the blood, then you did mine, and you plucked out some of the feathers and we wore them in our hair, behind our ears."

When he finishes, no one says anything. They sit in silence. Ray and Glenn look at him with dark faces.

Finally, Ray speaks. "That didn't happen, Jake."

"It did."

"I never killed any bird."

"You tore it apart, then you crushed its head."

"Maybe you were with someone else," Glenn says.

Jake shakes his head. He looks through the trees. In the distance he can see the man again, still hiding, still watching, but further away, like he's backtracking. "No," he says. "I was with you."

10

It is night. Jake changes into dark clothes and leaves the trailer, makes his way through the park. He is cautious. He takes his time. The moon and the stars are clouded over, their light snuffed. When Luann's trailer is in view he slows to a stop.

He will look in on her. Or he will smoke with her. They will attempt to recapture that night they shared, cigarettes and conversation until the early hours, until the sun begins to rise.

But she is not outside. She is not smoking. Ricky's truck is outside. Ricky is inside, with her.

Jake looks to Carlson's windows, checks them over, extra-vigilant so as not to be caught again. Satisfied that they are empty, that no one appears to be home, he takes a creeping step forward then halts. Someone is already at her trailer.

Jake watches. A round blob of a man presses himself against the panels, slides along and peers in every window. There is something in his hands. He lifts it to his face, then lowers it, looks at it, then lifts it to his face again.

Jake steps into the darkest shadows, gets closer. The fat man has a camera. He is taking pictures. Jake doesn't know what to do. The fat man looks familiar to him, but he does not know why.

The fat man goes stiff. His shoulders hunch up like he can feel Jake's eyes upon him. He spins quick. Their eyes meet. Jake holds out his hands, feels his jaw go slack. He wants to say it is all right, he is leaving, there is no need to worry, but then the fat man panics and makes to run, but he trips over a mooring and stumbles into the trailer, hits it hard, but he doesn't fall. He recovers himself, rolls against it, and takes off at a sprint down the back of the trailer, shockingly fast for a man so large.

The trailer door swings open. Light spills out, bathes the side of the parked truck. Ricky emerges, topless, his jeans look like they've been pulled on in a hurry – the belt is loose and the buttons are undone.

Jake stands very still, but it doesn't make a difference. Ricky's head snaps angrily from side to side, searching for the noise-making culprit, then settles on him. Jake knows he should run, knows he has to run, but his legs won't listen, and it is not until Ricky has jumped down the steps and is already pounding barefoot in his direction, issuing a guttural "*Hey!*" do his feet take heed and he spins, tries to run, but he can hear those heavy footfalls catching up, then they are right on top of him and he feels like a gazelle chased down by a lion, and Ricky tackles him to the ground. They roll, Jake ends up flat on his stomach, shards of grass between his teeth and dirt on his tongue. Ricky pulls his arm back, wrenches on it, pushes the side of his face into the ground.

"What the fuck d'you think you're doin, creep?" Ricky spits the words.

"You watchin us, motherfucker? That gettin you off?" He wrenches harder on the arm and Jake cries out.

"It wasn't me! It wasn't –"

Ricky doesn't listen. "Where's the camera? You were takin pictures, weren't you? I knew I saw somethin!"

"I swear –"

Ricky pulls him to his feet, keeps hold of his arm and his head, shoves him forward. "Show me where it is, you son of a bitch! Show me the fuckin camera!" He drags him back to Luann's trailer. She steps out, wrapped in a short nightgown.

"You get him, Ricky?" she calls, leaning out the open doorway, one hand clasping her robe closed.

"Yeah, I got him." Ricky dumps him on the ground, then grabs him by the hair and lifts his head so she can see his face. "You know him?"

Luann cocks her head to one side. A flicker of recognition crosses her face. She remembers sharing her cigarettes with him. Remembers talking with him. Remembers all the times she has seen him round school. "No," she says. "I don't know him."

Ricky pushes his face back into the dirt, then stands and kicks him in the ribs. Jake feels pain explode there, like his ribcage is going to split open, feels the wind rush out of him. He clutches at his side, gasps for breath.

"Jesus, Ricky!"

"He had a camera, Luann! This little freak was takin pictures of us!" He kicks Jake again, forces him onto his back, then pins him with a knee across his chest. "Where's the fuckin camera?" he says, then he punches him in the mouth. Jake can taste blood, his lips torn open against his teeth. "Where's the fuckin camera?" He hits him just below the eye. Jake feels fireworks go off in his skull.

He wants to open his mouth, to speak, to explain what has happened, who it really was, but he is knocked dizzy, his mouth won't work, it just hangs slack and fills with blood until he gags. He is aware of being hit again, maybe a couple more times, and he thinks he can hear a voice, a female's voice, Luann's voice – "Stop hittin him, Ricky! You're gonna kill him!"

And Ricky is talking, talking to Jake, ignoring Luann. "That what gets you off, huh? Watchin other people – takin pictures of them? You're sick, man, you're fuckin *sick*." There is another punch. It lands on the nose. Jake can hear things pop and crunch, but he doesn't feel them.

Then the hitting stops, the shouting stops, the weight is gone from his chest. Jake forces his eyes open, but only one – the right – will comply. The left is probably blackened, he reasons, from all the punching.

Two men are above him. Talking. Ricky is one of them. Jake tries to push himself up onto his elbow, so he can better see. Ricky gestures towards him on the ground, points sharply. Jake lies back down before Ricky notices he has moved. The other man holds up his hands, tries to calm the situation.

Jake hears the blood pounding in his ears, can't hear what they are saying. He looks at the other man, tries to see who it is. His vision is bleary with tears and blood. When he finally hears something, it is Luann's voice. "Ricky – come *on*."

Ricky turns to her.

"Just go," the other man says. "It's okay. I've got this."

It is Carlson. The other man is Carlson.

Ricky walks away.

Carlson waits until he is gone, until he and Luann are both inside, then reaches down and pulls Jake to his feet. "Can you walk?" he says. He grunts and wheezes as he wraps Jake's arm around his shoulder.

Jake's limbs feel like jelly. His consciousness feels separate to his body. "Whuh?"

Carlson drags him to his trailer, gets him inside and lies him down on the sofa. Jake stares at the fan on the ceiling. It is off. He is becoming aware of the various pains all over his body, primarily his face and head. The dull sensation that enveloped him during the beating is wearing off, everything is growing sharp.

With a groan, he manages to push himself upright, to a sitting position, but the back of his head rests against the wall and his eyes flutter. Carlson is in the kitchen, wetting one towel and using another to wrap ice. He brings them both over, uses the first to wipe away the blood, then gives the makeshift ice-pack to Jake to press where it hurts most.

"You wanna explain yourself?" Carlson says. "Because I'm pretty sure I warned you off this not so long ago."

Jake mumbles something. He can't get the words out. His tongue feels funny in his mouth, like he's bitten it.

"What?" Carlson says.

Jake escapes into sleep.

11

It is not a dream. It is a memory.

Down an alleyway off the main street. Homeless men and women occupy the shade of disused doorways, and the threat of violence lingers in the air mingling with the stink of piss and vomit and cheap booze and sweat. The bums watch passers-by through half-closed eyes like they're sizing them up, contemplating the contents of their pockets and their wallets, but they don't strike. They don't even beg. Their jaws work, toothless gums grind against each other, and this is worse. This inaction. It is as if they are taking mental photographs, formulating plans; as if they are about to become intrinsically entangled with the lives of the people they are watching. They are going to follow, to stalk, to watch and wait and when the moment is right and only when will they make their move. They are like snakes, coiled and ready and lightning fast. But they are patient.

There is one shop here, though it never looks open. The front is uninviting, as is the inside. The windows are covered with rusted metal grating, gaps in the glass where the posters on the inside are not overlapping. It is called the Back Alley Valley. It sells pornography.

Sometimes, they throw stuff out. Faulty DVD's, damaged books and magazines. They drop them in the dumpster outside and don't care if the bums retrieve them, use them for fire fuel or padding or personal gratification.

Jake and Ray and Glenn go to the dumpster. They search inside it, flick through the magazines they find. They have been inside the store but they were chased out. They were never going to buy anything, they were just going to shore up mental images for when they were alone, and to giggle amongst themselves at the more ludicrous things they found.

There is one magazine with a garish, almost comic book style cover featuring a dark-clad man lurking at the corner of a window frame, a young girl oblivious inside her room, getting dressed for bed. It is called '*Peepers, Prowlers, Pervs*'. It is as expected filled with naked women, fully naked, page after glossy page of them. Only a few of the shoots look like they've been professionally staged, with the women looking coquettishly down the camera lens, biting on a lip or a fingernail, playing with their hair or their nipples. For the most part, the women seem unaware, or at least play at being so. The pictures look like they've been taken through windows, catching them while they prepare for bed. Towards the back of the magazine there are pictures that have been shot through cars, catching couples sprawled naked across the backseats, doing things to each other. Some of the people, especially in these candid car shots, wear masks. Ray and Glenn point out the more ludicrous visages and laugh. The homeless people watch them, dozens of eyes unblinking in the shadows.

Ray finds another magazine. Its front cover is ominously dark with the title printed in white. It is called '*Murder Lust Magazine*'.

It is naked women again, but there is something different this time. There is a darker tone. There are no candid window shots. These people know they are being photographed. There are men in the pictures, too. Some people wear leather straps that criss-cross their torsos, and some – mainly the men – wear masks again.

The people are having sex. Angry sex. It is hard to tell if the women are enjoying it, or if they are in pain. Then, at the end of every shoot, someone is killed. Usually it is the women, but sometimes it is the men. There are stabbings, strangulations, there is one gunshot. Then there are close up images of the corpses. If it is a bloody death there are artful shots of the blood, pooling beneath the body or sprayed up the walls and across the ceiling. One woman licks an open head wound.

Ray and Glenn discuss whether or not the deaths are real. Jake looks through the window, through a gap in the posters. He can see a man behind the counter, an incredibly fat man, he talks to someone Jake can't see, shows him something. He laughs hard.

Jake knows he has seen him before.

The fat man kicked them out of the shop.

But before he kicked them out he showed them something, in a magazine, something Jake has tried to forget.

Jake imagines him with a camera in his hands.

Imagines him running away, disappearing into the dark.

Outside Luann's trailer.

12

Carlson's trailer is the same as the one Jake has grown up in. It is the same model. It has the same layout. But Carlson has kept his tidy. There are no unwashed clothes hanging over the backs of chairs; no empty bottles on the benches or in the middle of the floor; the surfaces are not coated in tobacco dust or particles of marijuana, and they are not marked with sticky rings where cans and bottles have stood in spilled alcohol. Carlson lives alone, and he keeps his home neat.

Two days have passed since Jake received the beating from Ricky. Carlson is usually at work. So far they have not seen much of each other. Jake keeps the curtains closed during the day and at night. He shuffles round the trailer in darkness. Everything hurts. He has searched the cupboards for painkillers but found none. There was beer in the fridge, so he drank it. It helped a little, but fleetingly so.

In the bathroom mirror, he inspects the damage. His left eye is closed, the top and bottom lids purple and bulging. Yellow-green bruising covers his face. His lips are cut and swollen. Flaps of skin hang loose on the insides of his cheeks. When he swallows he can taste blood. The taste puts him off food, for the most part, but when he does search for something to eat he finds nothing.

He sits and watches the television. Indecent Proposals. The fat loner is losing. The host is humiliating him. Jake turns it off. He goes to the window, bites his bloodied lip and peers out around the curtain, toward Luann's place, but sees nothing and quickly lets the curtain fall back into place.

When the pain gets too bad he lies on the sofa where he has slept the past two nights, and stares at the ceiling and wills sleep to come. He does not hurt when he is sleeping. He tells himself that when he is sleeping he is healing.

Last night he woke briefly when Carlson returned. Opened his eyes to see him locking the door after himself. He did not turn on the light. He stepped closer to Jake, leaned over with his head tilted to the side, listened as if he was checking his breathing. He didn't talk. When he was satisfied he turned away and went to the refrigerator. He looked inside then looked back over his shoulder at Jake and made a chuckling sound in the back of his throat. Jake figured he was looking for the beers. He closed the refrigerator door and made his way to his room, to bed. Jake promptly returned to sleep.

But when he tries to sleep, to escape the pain, it will not come. It stabs through his face and head like a million needles. He grits his teeth against it. He clenches his fists and stiffens his whole body and wishes he would stop hurting.

Carlson gets back late. He carries a grocery bag. Jake is not asleep, though he sits in darkness. Carlson sees him upright and turns on the light.

He nods, says "How're you feelin?"

"Like a million bucks."

Carlson grins with one side of his mouth. "You look it." He puts the bag down on the bench. "I brought food."

Jake sniffs. A new smell is in the air, but it does not come from the groceries. It is a greasy smell, of burgers and fries. Carlson has brought this smell in with him, and it lingers on him. "Where do you work?"

Carlson is busy putting things away. He pauses at Jake's question, turns his head. "I'm a chef," he says. "Well, maybe not so fancy. I'm a short-order cook. You ever been to Good Eats?"

"A couple of times."

"That's where I work."

Good Eats is on the far side of town, on the way out. Jake remembers that someone has spray painted a dragon on the wall outside. It is a very fine painting, and he thinks this is why no one has scrubbed it off.

Carlson finishes putting things away then stands at the counter. He moves very slowly, very deliberately. He rests his fists on top of the counter and leans forward. "Now. We need to talk about the other night."

Jake says nothing.

"You wanna explain yourself? Because I'm pretty sure I warned you off this kind of thing. And shit, when was it – like three days before you got beat up or somethin?"

"It wasn't me."

Carlson looks him up and down. Jake is still wearing the same clothes. All black. "Uh-huh."

Jake could protest, could tell him that he knows who it was – the fat man with the camera, and he knows where he works – but he doubts Carlson would believe him so he doesn't bother. He doubts anyone would believe him.

"So you like to look in on young ladies, huh? Just her over the way, or are there more?"

"No. Just her."

"Then tell me what's so special about her."

Jake opens his mouth but finds that the adequate words escape him. Instead, he manages "I know her."

"You know her."

"Yes."

"What – you're friends?"

"I know her from school."

Carlson raises an eyebrow. "Does she know you?"

"Yes."

"How well?"

Jake hesitates. "Enough."

Carlson crosses his arms. "So what's the deal, Jake? You think she's the *one* or some bullshit like that? Two of you ever get together you've got a real meet-cute goin on there – boy meets girl, boy peeps obsessively through girl's window while she's entertainin, girl finally realises it's the stalker she really wants to be with and not the Mr Muscles she's been shackin up with."

Jake looks away.

"That what you want?"

"I don't know what I want."

"Maybe I'm just gettin old, but she looked way too thin to me. She the most beautiful girl you laid eyes on?"

"I dunno – there's more to it than just looks –"

"I'm sure she's got a winnin personality."

"Why do you care?"

"Because like some damn fool you're gonna get yourself killed just because you can't stop yourself from lookin in through her windows."

"Are you gonna tell my dad?"

"No, I ain't gonna tell him. But I don't see how you're gonna keep it secret with your face all messed up like it is."

"I'll just…I'll stay somewhere else until it heals. He won't notice I'm gone."

"Where you gonna stay?"

"I got friends…"

"What about their parents? They won't say anythin to your pa?"

Jake shrugs.

Carlson lets out a long breath. He looks off to one side, scratches the back of his neck. Jake hasn't seen him in the light before. He is not a tall man, just a few inches on Jake, and thin, his cheeks and eyes sunken in his face. His hair is shaved close to the skull, and his skin is leathery tough. Age-wise he is about the same as Harry.

"You can stay here. Least until the worst of the swelling goes down."

Jake chews a loose flap of skin on his bottom lip. "Why?"

"Why what?"

"Why would you let me do that?"

"Ain't a man alive that hasn't tried to avoid a thrashin from his daddy at some time or other. I'm just offering you a way to do so."

"I don't know you."

"That's true. I'll understand if you say no. Hell son, it's no skin off my back, believe me. I'm just tryin to do you a good turn. If you wanna walk out then you go right ahead, I won't stop you."

Jake looks past Carlson, to the door. Carlson steps aside, clears the way. Jake thinks about Harry. Thinks about Maggie. Thinks about Maggie's dress. Thinks about the noises he'd heard her make, in his father's room.

"Okay," he says.

"Okay what?"

"I'll stay here."

Carlson nods. "Okay. But you leave that damn girl alone, y'hear?"

Jake nods.

Carlson looks at him for a long time. The muscles in his cheek dance as he grits his teeth, looks like he's thinking something over. "Well then, now I need to ask you a question."

"Sure."

"Are you a virgin?"

"Whuh – what?"

Carlson shifts his weight from one foot to the other, looks uncomfortable, but he perseveres. "Have you ever had sex?"

"Why?"

"Just answer."

"What's it got to do with you? It's none of your damn business."

"I guess that's probably a no."

"I didn't say that –"

"Then say *Yes*."

Carlson looks away, says nothing.

"Look, Jake, I ain't tryin to embarrass you here. I'm askin for a reason. This whole peepin business, it needs to stop. You don't wanna take another beatin like the one you took the other night – ain't always gonna be someone there to get the other guy off of you. Could be one day someone comes chargin out with a shotgun – reckon you could outrun that? You couldn't outrun me, you didn't even hear me comin. Somethin like this, we gotta nip it in the bud before it gets you in trouble, or hurt. You know what they do when a dog's aggressive?"

"They put it down."

"Well, sometimes. Or they get it laid. That evens it out. Now, we ain't gonna get you put down, so I'm figurin if we get you laid that'll straighten you out, get this whole peepin nonsense outta your head."

Jake snorts.

"You think it's stupid?"

Jake shifts in his seat. "Maybe. I dunno. But I mean, who's gonna – who would even wanna sleep with me? I ain't got anyone lined up or nothin."

Carlson scratches the back of his neck. His face is conflicted, looks like he is still trying to decide whether this is a good idea or not. Finally, he says "I know someone."

13

Jake has sneaked peeks at Luann's trailer every night. Ricky has not returned. His truck never pulls up. Jake wants to go outside, creep over and look in and see what she is doing, but he can't. He's scared.

He has been with Carlson for more than a week, almost two. The wounds to his face have mostly healed. The swelling has gone down, the cuts are closing, but the days are long and boring and Carlson is rarely there and his only company is the television and he stares at it absently and pulls the scabs from his lips and tastes blood in his mouth and a sting when the peeling dead flesh meets fresh.

"Where've you been?" Glenn asks.

Jake shrugs. He has not prepared an excuse. "Ill," he says.

"What was wrong?"

"Flu." Jake thinks of the headache Rick's beating gave him, the aches that ran through his body. "It felt like flu."

Glenn pulls up his collar to cover his mouth. "Well don't be spreadin it to me."

"Are you better now?" Ray says. He takes a step back.

"I'm fine," Jake says. "I'm fine."

It is dark and the marks on his face have faded enough so as to be unnoticeable. When he left Carlson's trailer he crept out like he was breaking curfew, went round the back and made his escape into town through the woods as if fearing that anyone who might see him would report back. Most importantly, he did not want Luann to see him. He was confident that she did not.

He found Ray and Glenn at the back of the empty warehouse. It was too dark to skate so they threw stones at the windows, saw who could smash the most, and the highest, and who could make the better shots. Ray won. Glenn blamed it on his height. "B-baller's arms," he said. "Unfair advantage."

They walk through town, carrying their skateboards. For Jake it feels good to be out of the trailer, off the trailer park. It feels good to be with his friends, and for them not to know what has happened to him. They go into a takeaway and Ray buys a box of mixed meat and Glenn gets fries but Jake has no money and he gets nothing. They sit on their skateboards outside and Jake sits on the kerb and Glenn shares his fries and Ray shovels the meat into his mouth with his right hand and chews with his mouth open. Grease runs down his chin. On his fingers it catches the light of the flickering streetlamp nearby, it glistens. Something crunches in his mouth and he spits out a bone but he doesn't seem to care.

When he finishes eating, Ray says, "Glenn and Kelly broke up."

Glenn hits him on the arm.

"What happened?" Jake says.

Glenn shrugs. "Just didn't work out is all."

"She's getting her braces off in a couple of weeks," Ray says. "Glenn told her he couldn't wait, because then she'd be able to suck his dick."

Glenn hits him again, harder this time, and in the ribs. Ray doubles over, winded and laughing. "Shut up, man!"

"Did you think she'd like that?" Jake says.

"Actually, yeah, yeah I did. I thought it was, like, dirty talk, y'know. I thought it would, kinda, turn her on."

"But it didn't."

"No it did not."

"She broke up with you."

Ray laughs.

"Fuck you, too. I thought at least one a you two fuckers might've been a little sympathetic."

"*Sorry,*" Ray says, but he does not sound sorry.

"I guess it's hard for either of you to be understanding when neither of you have popped that cherry yet, huh?" Glenn says. He grins wickedly.

Ray shrugs. "Workin on it," he says. He's still smirking.

"You could always go to the motel, see the hooker."

Jake goes stiff. He looks the other way but his friends don't notice. They are too busy bickering between themselves.

"Shit, maybe I will," Ray says. "Nothin stopping me."

"You do that. Anyway, Kelly's gonna come round, I know she will. She likes me too much."

"You're sure of that, huh?"

"Hell, I know it."

Ray gets to his feet. "Whatever, man." He grins. "But hey, don't be one a those losers that spends their life pining after the girl that got away, all right? Shit, you're already boring enough as it is."

Glenn stands too, shoves him, threatens to hit him with his skateboard. "Fuck you." But they're both smiling.

Jake stands, joins them. They start walking. "Where are we going?" he says.

"Don't know," Ray says.

They walk. They end up at the park, go through it. They pass a trembling, panting bush. Glenn hits them both on the arm to slow down, then presses a finger to his lips for them to be quiet. He creeps over closer to the bush then pounces on it and shakes its branches and roars like a Grizzly.

The couple in the bush start cursing loudly. "The fuck're you doin, man? Get outta here!" The voice is male, young.

"Fuckin kids!" says another voice, male, older.

Glenn and Ray laugh and they leave the bush and continue through the park. A homeless man in tattered clothes stumbles past them, he supports himself on a bending golf club turned upside down, its head clutched in his hand. He drags his left foot and his mouth hangs open, spit dangles from the corner, and his eyes are nearly closed. He looks strung out on something and he stinks of weeks-old sweat. As he passes he tilts a hat he is not wearing and says "Evenin, fellas."

A man sleeps on one of the benches encircling the water feature. He wears a long overcoat, its tattered tail touching the ground, and he has a beard thick enough it looks like birds nest in it. Ray and Glenn whisper conspiratorially then lean their skateboards against the water feature and go over to him, start piling rubbish on top of him. They laugh behind their hands. They put newspapers on him, then bottles and cans, burger tissues and a black banana skin. Ray finds an old condom amidst all the dead leaves and he puts it on the man's shoulder and Glenn walks away biting on the inside of his elbow so as not to wake the man with his laughter. Tears stream from his eyes down his red face. Ray bites his lip, his shoulders shaking, gathers up an armful of leaves and drops them onto the man.

He wakes with a start, calls out incoherently, flaps his arms so all the rubbish falls off him and now Ray and Glenn laugh openly. He wheels on the three and launches himself at them and Ray and Glenn scatter but Jake stays where he is, feeling like a detached observer, as if this whole thing has been something watched on a television screen, but then the bearded man has him by the shoulders and he's garbling inarticulately and his eyes are narrowed like he means to do something bad but then Ray hits him in the back of the head with his skateboard and he lets go of Jake and falls to his knees then Glenn swings his own skateboard and strikes him in the right side with the hard edge, down his shoulder and ribs and he falls and Ray hits him on the back then Glenn hits him in the back and side of the head and Jake can see blood at his ear, either coming from inside the ear or the outside it is hard to tell, but then Ray kicks the man and they leave him.

"The fuck was his problem?" Glenn says, breathless, as they walk away.

14

Carlson drives them in his truck to the motel. It is not far from the trailer park. He pulls into one of the bays of the mostly empty car park, tells Jake to stay where he is. "I'll be right back," he says.

He gets out of the truck, makes his way across the forecourt and up a flight of steps. At the top he continues, passes a couple of doors then knocks on the one at the end. He goes inside. The door closes.

Jake looks round. It has been a long time since he was last at the motel, but he's never been here at night. It is late and it is dark and most of the building is in shadow. It feels like a dozen pairs of eyes are watching him from the darkened windows. His skin crawls. He shifts in his seat. He looks round like he expects people are going to crawl out of the black and start climbing over the cab of the truck, try to get inside, to get at him.

There is light at the reception, the only room that seems to be lit. A man sits behind the desk. Tall, pale, long black hair. It is hard to tell from the distance, but Jake thinks he is watching the truck. He barely moves, like a statue. Jake feels uncomfortable. He doesn't like being here at night. There is something horror movie creepy about the place. Something just below the surface that unnerves him.

Carlson leaves the room, comes down the stairs, crosses to the truck. He opens Jake's door. "Come on," he says.

Jake has butterflies in his stomach. His mouth is dry. He realises how nervous he is. He knows why they have come to this place, that he is going to – about to – lose his virginity. The whole thing has been planned for days now. "Where?" he says. He doesn't know why he asks. He knows where they are going – the same room Carlson just left.

"Where do you think we're goin? Come on." Carlson takes a step back, holds the door a little wider. Still, Jake does not move. "Are you nervous?"

Jake looks into the darkness that surrounds the motel.

"It's all right to be nervous, Jake. But you ain't gotta be worried. Come on. I'll walk you in. You'll be fine."

Jake takes a deep breath.

"But I ain't gonna hold your hand," Carlson says. "Afraid I'm gonna have to draw the line at that."

Jake manages a weak laugh, gets out the truck. Carlson slams the door, then leads him up the steps. They go to room number sixteen. Next to the door is a cowboy spray-painted onto the wall. Lee Van Cleef in 'Death Rides a Horse'. Carlson sees him looking at it.

"Last time I was here," he says, "that paintin wasn't there."

"When was the last time?"

"Other week."

Jake thinks about the dragon on the side of Good Eats. "Who did it?"

"I don't know. I don't think it was commissioned." Carlson knocks on the door to room sixteen then pushes on the handle, doesn't wait for a response. Jake follows him in.

The room smells stale, like Harry's room, but a different kind of stink. This isn't alcohol sweat. Jake doesn't know what it is, but he thinks it might be sex.

"This is him?" She is on the bed, sitting. Jake didn't realise she was there until she spoke.

"Yeah," Carlson says.

"How old did you say he was?"

"He's eighteen."

She doesn't look like she believes him. "Sure," she says.

"Is it gonna be a problem?"

"If he's eighteen? No. No problem."

"You're gettin paid, ain't you?"

"There's no problem."

Carlson turns to Jake. "This is Joanie," he says.

Jake can't meet her eyes, but he manages to nod in her direction.

"What happened to your face?" Joanie says.

"Nothin wrong with his face," Carlson says.

"Not anymore. But there're cuts, I can see them."

"You got good eyes, Joanie. He fell," Carlson says. "At work. He tripped."

"That right? Where's he work?"

"At the diner. He's a waiter."

"I've never seen him."

"He's new."

"He can't tell me that himself?"

"He don't talk much."

"You shy, sweetie?" Joanie says.

Jake shifts his feet.

"He's all right," Carlson says.

"You can leave now," Joanie says.

"Sure," Carlson says. "I'll be right outside."

Jake stares at the ground. Carlson gives him a slap on the back, then leaves the room. Joanie stays on the bed.

"This your first time?" she says.

Jake clears his throat but that doesn't make it any easier to speak.

"You wanna come over here and sit with me?"

His feet won't move.

"You don't need to be shy with me, sweetie. I'll take care of you. There's no rush. We can take our time."

Jake's jaw is clenched tight. It begins to cramp.

Joanie gets off the bed, goes to him. Jake looks at her out the corner of his eye. She is of about his height, but she is very thin, painfully so. She wears loose clothes – a white vest and blue shorts – that she probably sleeps in. The room is dark save for a lamp in the corner, the bulb weak. The sheets on the bed are creased, look like they haven't been cleaned or changed in a while, though probably they look that way because so many bodies have lain upon them.

She takes his hands in hers, leads him over to the bed, sits him down. Her hands are soft, but bony. She sits beside him with one leg crossed under herself. "Carlson told me your name's Jake," she says.

He nods.

"You ever talk?"

He shrugs again.

She laughs. "You don't need to be scared, sweetie. You wanna take your clothes off?"

He goes stiff. She notices.

"You want maybe I should take mine off first?"

Jake sits very still, like he hopes she can only register movement in the dark and she'll forget he is there and he'll be able to creep away. Except Carlson is still outside, and Carlson will expect the deed to have been done.

Joanie stands, takes off her clothes, lets them drop to her feet. "There," she says. "I told you. It's nothin to be afraid of."

Jake snatches glances. Without the clothes it's like he can see every bone in her body. The only parts of her that look fleshy are her breasts, but they sag like balloons that have been deflated. The hair at her crotch is thick and dark, it hides her genitalia from view, and when she raised her arms to pull the vest over her head he'd noticed dark patches at her armpits too.

She reaches out. "Let me help you," she says.

Jake goes limp. He doesn't fight it. Lets her take off his jacket, then roll his t-shirt up over his head. She goes down to her knees to undo the buckle of his jeans, and he becomes very aware of how hard he is breathing, and the angry drumbeat of his heart, the dryness in his mouth.

Between his legs, she takes off his pants. He sits in his underwear, nothing else. His skin pricks with a coldness that isn't there. When her fingers touch him he feels electricity pulse from the point of contact, course through him. While her face is turned down, away from his, he looks at her. She is plain, devoid of make-up, her features framed by the lank hair that falls either side of her head. There is a tiredness to her. Despite her soft talk and her assurances, despite the way she calls him '*sweetie*' and makes out like they are going to be the best of friends, this is just a job to her. She is going through the motions. This isn't her first-time with a virgin. She's been through this all before, so many times.

She presses her hand against his crotch, through his boxer shorts. There is a burst of pleasure and Jake closes his eyes. He is hard and hot against her. Through the thin fabric she grips him firmly. Jake bites his lip. She raises her face, puts her mouth to his ear.

"You just lie back, sweetie," she says. "Joanie's gonna do all the work."

He does as she says, twisting his body so his head is at the top of the bed. Joanie peels off his underwear, drops it to one side. Jake stares at the stained ceiling. He sees a bug crawl across it, scuttling slowly. Joanie opens a drawer by the side of the bed. Jake turns his head to look. From the drawer she has taken lubricant, she squeezes it onto the tips of her fingers then sits on the edge of the bed, rubs it into herself. She reaches into the drawer again, puts the tube back, searches for something else. Jake can hear a packet rustle. When she takes her hand out she holds a condom. She removes it from the foil then puts it on him. Jake's back arches at her touch, his head goes deeper into the sweat-stained pillows.

The condom on, she holds him by the base and climbs on top, eases him into her artificial moisture. Jake groans, grits his teeth and clenches his fists. His whole body is stiff. Waves of ecstasy run through him, up and down his limbs and in his stomach, make his breath catch. Joanie presses her body against him, her small breasts flat against his chest. She holds him tight and bounces her hips, and Jake can feel, though he fights against it, that this is not going to last very long.

He finishes with a choked cry, his tight body goes limp on the bed, feels like he is pumping so much fluid into the condom it is sure to burst. The act complete, business done, Joanie gets off him, off the bed, steps to one side, grabs her clothes from the floor and puts them back on.

Aware of his nudity, and despite everything still embarrassed by it, Jake rolls onto his side, his back to her, struggles to pull off the condom. He swings his legs over the edge of the mattress, sits up to better get at it. It isn't as full as he'd expected it to be. Off, pinched between his fingers, he doesn't know what to do with it. There is a wastebasket nearby.

"Put a knot in it," Joanie says.

He flinches, does as she says, drops it into the basket. There are tissues there, but no condoms. Joanie throws his clothes onto the bed beside him. He flinches again, won't turn, won't look at her, picks his items of clothing up one at a time and pulls them on, starts with his underwear.

"Told you I'd be gentle," Joanie says. "You gonna talk to me now?"

Jake gets dressed, self-conscious. He knows she is watching him. When he doesn't respond she doesn't talk to him again. Fully clothed, he sits there, his back still to her, not sure what to do next, wondering if he should just leave. He wants to turn, to talk to her, to say *something*.

Looking back, she isn't there. The bulb is on in the bathroom, its light shining out through the open door. He didn't hear her go in there, but his concentration while redressing had been deafening.

He stands, looks to the door. It would be easy to go, to just leave. He doesn't need to say anything to her, and she has afforded him this opportunity to make his escape. No doubt she senses his trepidation, his nerves and shyness. Making for the door, he gets as far as the foot of the bed, stops, turns back and goes into the bathroom's light and sees her at the open window, her back to him, blowing cigarette smoke out into the darkness. In the light he can see that her underwear is marked with stains he doesn't want to think about. Her bare pale legs are dotted with bruises and a couple of small scratches. On her right ass cheek, barely covered by her underwear, there is a red bruise that has the shape of a handprint. Her right leg is bent slightly at the knee, and as he watches her she shifts her weight, straightens out her right leg and bends the left. If she feels his eyes on her she does not turn.

Jake steps into the bathroom, stands in the doorway. The bathroom is very clean. It doesn't smell like the rest of the motel room. It smells of bleach.

Joanie spares him a glance. "You're still here?"

He swallows. "Yeah."

She raises an eyebrow, turns, blows smoke and looks him up and down. She offers him a cigarette. "Smoke?"

He takes one, puts it between his lips and she lights it for him. He coughs.

"*Do* you smoke?"

"Regularly." He blows a ring. Opening his mouth, talking to her, it seems so easy now, like there is nothing to it, like there has never been any need to be afraid and shamed and nervous and scared, he opens his mouth and the words come, his voice is heard.

"You don't really work with him, do you? With – him outside, I forget his name."

"Carlson."

"What is he, your dad?"

"No. He's a friend of my dad."

"How old are you really?"

"Sixteen."

She laughs. "Shit." She takes a long draw from the cigarette. "Why didn't your dad bring you along?"

"He doesn't know."

"You've got a strange situation, sweetie."

"I know."

"At least you're talking now."

"It's a breakthrough."

She smiles. "What happened to your face?"

"I got hit."

"How'd the other guy come off?"

"There ain't a mark on him."

"You have it coming?"

He shrugs. "Probably."

"Everybody does, right?"

Jake steps to the window and looks down. In the dark he sees movement, a man and a dog, two silhouettes passing through the night. Joanie finishes her cigarette and drops what is left out the window. She presses her hand to Jake's cheek and he looks at her, looks her in the eye. "Next time try and find a girl your own age, huh? You're not always gonna have a Carlson round to pay for you, and trust me, you don't wanna start payin for it. You'll never stop."

Jake sucks on the cigarette then throws it out the window, nods at her.

She smiles at him, lets her hand fall from his face. "You better get goin," she says. "You stay in here any longer he's gonna get jealous, start thinkin you're some kind of marathon man."

"Okay."

When he is nearly at the door she speaks again. "Remember what I said, sweetie."

Outside, as the door closes, Carlson turns from the railing, looks him over. "There's a change," he says. "A definite change. I can see it. Look at you, chest all puffed out, shoulders all square." He grins, leans a little closer. "And what's that I smell – a post-coitus cigarette? Tasted good, didn't it?" He laughs, slaps Jake on the arm. "You did good, kid. You wanna tell me about it?"

Jake is tongue-tied again, that earlier ease of conversation he'd shared with Joanie gone.

"Ah, that's okay. Keep it to yourself. You feel good?"

"Yeah. Yeah, I do."

Carlson smiles. He looks like a proud parent. He reaches out, squeezes Jake's shoulder. "That's great. Come on. Let's go back."

15

Jake stands at the back of the trailer, smokes. It is night and Carlson is at work. Jake could leave the park, go into town, find Ray and Glenn, but he doesn't. He doesn't want to be stuck inside the trailer, but nor does he want to be with his friends. His mind is preoccupied. Being with them would fill him with an impatient giddiness, make him jittery until he'd feel as if he was about to explode.

Instead, he thinks about Joanie. About the sex.

He'd expected the loss of his virginity to bring on a noticeable change, but it has not. The horniness, the desperation for sex, has not faded. If anything, it has increased. Joanie infests his thoughts, possesses him, she is in his dreams and his blood and she will not go away. It is a need that must be satisfied, but it is a need that requires money. He does not have any money.

Dead cigarettes pile at his feet as he chain smokes, works his way through the pack. There are only a few left. He looks into the woods, into the gap between the trees. Sees shadows move. Animals or men, he can't tell. He can feel eyes. Can see two pinpoints of glinting light peering at him from behind a tree. He stares back and flicks another smoked cigarette and thinks about Joanie on top, the way she bounced, the way her skin pressed against his. She was not young, she looked worn and tired, but she felt so soft and smooth against him. He feels the blood pool in his crotch.

"Hey."

He gives a start, straightens up and looks to the right. Feels his face flush. It is Luann. He nods but says nothing.

She smiles weakly, looks sheepish. "I didn't expect to see you here."

"Then why're you here?"

She frowns, jerks her thumb back at her trailer. "Folks are home," she says. "I didn't feel like bein round them."

Jake blows smoke.

"How're you doing?" she says.

"Fine."

She takes a tentative step closer. "Your face looks good," she says. "Last time I saw you...there was a lotta blood."

"Mm."

She bites her lip. "Got one spare?" She indicates the cigarette between his lips.

He takes it from his mouth and hands it to her. It is new, barely smoked. He gets himself another, lights it.

"I've been wanting to talk to you," she says. She trails off, looks at his face and bites her lip again but can't hold his gaze and looks away, towards the trees.

Jake smokes and says nothing. Seeing her reminds him of Ricky, of the attack. The blows rain down on him again, their impact fresh in his mind. His head aches and his eyes feel as though they are swelling closed. He can taste blood.

His cheeks burn, remembering. It angers him. She, here, right now, trying to talk to him, angers him. "Where's Ricky?" he says. He tries not to spit it.

"We broke up," she says. "After...after what he did to you."

He raises an eyebrow. "Should I be grateful?"

"You can be whatever you want. He went too far."

"Why'd you want to talk to me?"

"To say sorry. For what he did." Her voice hardens at his belligerence. "But he said you were looking in."

Jake shakes his head, looks her in the eye. "I wasn't looking."

"You were the only one there."

"No, I wasn't. But it doesn't matter what I say, because I *was* there. The other guy got away. That's why no one saw him. Your boyfriend was too busy beating on me."

Luann blows smoke. Despite the cold she wears denim cut-offs and a grey vest, the sleeves of her jacket are knotted around her waist. Her hair is tied back but a few loose strands hang down her face. "I said sorry."

"You didn't do it."

"Where were you going?"

He lies. "I was just passing. Truth be told, I was hopin you were outside, like the last time." But it is not a complete lie. There is truth in that. Deep down, more than looking in on her he'd wanted nothing more than for her to be sat outside, exiled by her parents' noise. "Remember that? I was hopin to talk to you again. I liked it. I liked talkin with you." He wants her to feel bad.

Her face drops a little and he sees he has been successful. "Why didn't you say anythin, about the other guy?" Her voice is softer.

Jake shrugs. "What difference would it make. It's done now."

There is movement in the bushes amongst the trees. A bird takes flight, caws loudly as it goes. Luann looks but Jake does not. He inhales deeply on his cigarette, looks Luann up and down while she is distracted, and feels nothing. He looks at her and his face hurts with the memory of another's fists. The desire for her, the need, it is gone. In its place, his blood boils.

He straightens up, steps away, dumps the cigarette down with the rest of them. "I've gotta get goin," he says.

Luann looks back. "Oh," she says. "Okay."

The thought crosses his mind that he could invite her to walk with him, and they could go somewhere else together rather than the place he has in mind, but he quashes it. He clings to his anger. "Goodbye," he says, and he says it like this is the last time they'll see each other.

"Bye," she says, and does not move as he passes.

He walks fast, rounds trailers until he is out of view of her, then he starts to run. He runs until he is off the trailer park and heading toward the town, toward its lights, and his legs burn and his chest burns and he's breathing hard, wheezing, and the cold gets in his eyes so they start to water and he reaches town and keeps running, keeps running until he reaches his mother's street and then he stops and he hides in shadows and bends over to catch his breath but his eyes are fixed on her house, on the lights that burn brightly in the upstairs windows.

He spits hard and waits until he doesn't feel like he's going to throw up anymore then he searches the ground until he finds a stone large enough to do some real damage, to make more than a few scratches on the side of her car, then goes up to the house and notices with satisfaction that her car is still scarred, it hasn't been repaired yet, and he goes down the side of the house and he stands in the middle of her back yard and he throws the stone through a dark downstairs window, he doesn't know which room, maybe the kitchen or maybe the family room, and the glass shatters inwards and before they inside can register what has happened he is running, he runs back through the town and out of the town and back towards the waiting darkness of the trailer park.

16

Room sixteen. He watches the door, standing in the shadows out of the glow of the streetlamps where he could be seen. Whenever a car pulls in he conceals himself behind a column, pokes his head out from around it to continue his vigil.

He watches the men that go up the stairs and make that short walk to her room. To room sixteen. They knock. Sometimes they have to wait. Usually they don't. They are never in for very long. Jake doesn't recognise any of the men. Some of them look drunk. They sway from side to side, stumble up the steps.

He grits his teeth. He has no money. He wishes he did.

The notion crosses his mind to go to her door anyway, expectant of the look on her face when she opens it and sees him standing there. Surprise at first, then it will turn into a smile. She will invite him inside. They don't have to fuck. They can just talk. Turn out the lights and sit cross-legged on the floor beside her bed where no one can see them through the windows, and ignore the men that come and knock, make sure to have locked the door so it doesn't open when they try the handle after they receive no response. They just have to talk. She can make him feel good again, the way she did last time.

He doesn't go knock. The fear of the reality crushes him. He cannot knock upon her door without money in his pocket.

He steps back, deeper into the shadows, presses himself against the wall, unsure why he can't leave, what he is waiting for, what he expects to happen.

He thinks about his mother. He can't remember much about her. Doesn't even know why she left, and Harry won't talk about it.

She was always so secretive, always in another room. As a child he sat upon Harry's knee and they watched old war movies and cowboy movies and laughed together and pointed finger guns at the screen but she never joined them. She was reading, maybe. Or packing her things to leave.

She crept out in the early morning. Jake missed school that day. She never woke him. He went into her room, yawning, and saw the bed was empty. Harry had already left for work. She must have waited until he was gone, then gathered up her things and fled. Jake didn't understand what was happening. He sat and watched television and waited for someone to come back. He got hungry. He ate cereal.

Harry returned late. He smelled of beer. He looked at Jake with narrowed eyes, said "Where's your mother?"

He stormed round the trailer like it was five times bigger than it was, like there was somewhere in it she could feasibly hide, kept shouting "*Patti! Patti!*" until his throat was raw and he couldn't talk for a few days after.

She'd left no note. She didn't try to make contact. She never came back.

Anything she hadn't taken with her that day she left behind. Harry didn't keep any of it. Clothes, mostly. He took them outside and burned them.

Jake thinks about her new husband, and her new children. Wonders if she was having an affair.

A truck pulls into the forecourt. Three men get out. They talk loudly, like they've been drinking, but they don't look drunk. They go up the stairs. Jake holds his breath. They go to room sixteen. They have to take turns. One at a time. The other two wait outside, joke and laugh, until the door opens and they can rotate. Jake feels sick.

"Who are you?"

Jake starts, but he forces himself to turn casually. A dark face peers at him from the shadows, two unblinking eyeballs trained upon him, the whites incredibly bright.

"I don't know your face." The voice is deep and measured.

Jake clears his throat. "I have a room."

"Which one?"

He nods his head at the nearest door. "This one."

The face comes closer, looks into his eyes then studies the rest of his features, then sniffs him. The face smiles, teeth as white as the eyes. "Are you waiting for the woman?"

"No."

The smile broadens. "Then what are you waiting for?"

"I'm not waiting for anything. I'm just gettin some air."

"Of course." The face, the eyes and the mouth, stay where they are for a long moment, the smile never fading until it begins to make Jake nervous. "You will be waiting a long time if you don't get in the queue." Then the man turns and leaves without another word, makes his way down past the rooms and disappears.

Jake frowns, watches him go, shrugs him off as a resident motel oddity, then turns back to room sixteen to see that the three men have returned to their truck, they are pulling out, driving off. As they go, a man enters the motel's lights. He makes his way towards the steps. Jake grits his teeth, clenches his fists. It is Carlson. He goes up to room sixteen. He knocks twice, then goes inside.

Jake spits, punches the column but this does not satisfy him so be punches it again and feels his knuckles split and blood begin to flow from between his fingers. He stares at the door to room sixteen like he could tear it off its hinges, set fire to everything inside.

Before he leaves he looks into the reception. The pale man with long hair is there, he stands at the glass. He is looking at Jake. Watching him.

17

Jake takes a detour back to the trailer park. He goes via his mother's street. It is so late there are no lights on in the windows. He wants to go round the back and inspect the damage to the window but he does not.

He knows that one day they will install a security camera, to catch their phantom vandal, but he doesn't care.

On the way up the path leading to their front door he unzips himself, pulls out his penis, and when he gets to the door he pisses on it, makes sure to get plenty on the door handle, then he puts himself away and goes back to Carlson's trailer.

18

The man on the screen wipes at his eyes behind his spectacles after every question. He is short, balding, sports a weak, patchy beard. He wears a paisley shirt and the armpits are wet, and spreading.

Jake eats a sandwich and watches. The couple are winning. The couples always win.

They are young. The guy looks like a clean-cut realtor straight out of a football scholarship sponsored trip to college; the girl looks like a clean-cut homemaker fresh out of a head-cheerleader, prom queen, straight-A journey through high school. The both of them are all blonde hair and blue eyes and big white pearly smiles. The presenter mocks the singleton, and the couple laugh heartily.

"It's looking like a runaway victory!" the presenter says. "Are you going to put up any kind of fight?"

The singleton mumbles.

"Can't hear you, pal! You really need to work on your lines – no wonder you're here playing solo!"

The man on the television, the singleton, keeps coughing, he clears his throat. He speaks. His voice is very quiet, barely audible. "You're all horrible people," he says.

"Oh, come on, don't be like that!" the presenter says.

The singleton puts his hand in his pocket. "You're bullies," he says.

"It's just a game, pal! It's just a bit of fun! Hey, you could still turn it all round!" He winks at the screen.

"No." The man takes his hand from his pocket. "I can't." He holds scissors. He jams them into his neck. Blood sprays.

The presenter panics. "Shit!"

The young couple scream.

The camera cuts away to the audience, shows them jumping to their feet, some of them flee up the aisles, most of them lean closer to get a better look.

The camera cuts off, the screen goes black. It cuts to commercials. Jake eats his sandwich. Indecent Proposals does not return. A Mexican soap opera begins. He watches it.

19

Jake knocks on his mother's door. It is daytime, before twelve. Her husband has gone to work – Jake watched him leave, watched his car pull out and drive off – and her replacement children are at a friend's house.

It takes her a long time to answer, probably caught off guard, not expecting any visitors. When she finally does get to the door he doesn't wait for her to look him up and down, doesn't wait for her to remember who he is.

"Do you recognise me?"

His voice is hard. His mother looks thrown.

Patti. *Patti*. Her name is Patti.

Patti looks into his face and there is alarm in her eyes. There is fear. "Jacob," she says.

He nods fiercely. "That's right. Thought you woulda forgotten all about me by now." His mouth is dry in his fury. He licks his lips, still with so much to say. "Tried your damnedest, didn't you?"

Her mouth opens and closes but she struggles to find the words. She has gone very pale.

Jake holds out his arms. "Ain't you gonna ask me how I been?" He is enjoying her discomfort.

"What – how – how did you find me?"

Jake laughs. "That's what you wanna know?"

Patti holds the door like she is about to slam it in his face, but she won't. All colour, all strength, has been drained from her. She looks limp, tired, as if that hand on the door is all that keeps her upright. "What are you doing here?"

"That's better, that's more like it – I want something. That a surprise to you? You owe me a hell of a lot."

"You smashed the windows," she says quietly.

"And I've scratched your cars and pissed on your house and more besides. Give me what I want and I'll stop."

"I can call the police."

Jake laughs in her face, a harsh sound that is more like a dog's bark. "Go ahead. Call the cops. Call them on your abandoned firstborn. What d'you think Harry will do when he finds out?"

She swallows and her face goes paler, though he hadn't thought it possible.

"All I gotta do, is give him an address."

"What do you want?" It's barely a whisper.

"I want money."

She doesn't look surprised.

"Fifty bucks."

She looks surprised. Her eyes narrow. "What are you going to do with fifty bucks?"

"I'm going to fuck a prostitute."

Patti reels as if she has been struck.

Jake lifts his chin. "Run along and get it now. You ain't got it in the house I'll be more'n happy to wait. I don't mind. I got nowhere else I need to be."

Patti moistens her lips. "Then what?" she says.

"What do you mean?"

"You're gonna keep coming back here, demanding money, that it?"

Jake runs his tongue round the inside of his mouth. "Nah. This one time, then we'll call it even."

"*Even*'?"

"*Even* on account of what a no-good piece of shit mother you been to me, and I don't want to ever have to talk to you again." He catches his breath. "Standing here like this, face to face with you, I get that now. I understand it. All this time I've been angry at you for leaving me behind, but now I'm just angry. I thought maybe talkin to you I wouldn't feel that way, like maybe I'd be a kid again just wishin his mommy would come back and get him. But I don't. Now, go and get my fuckin money."

Patti lets go of the door but she does not fall. She turns and walks deeper into the house and Jake can see as she goes that her hands are shaking.

He turns away while he waits and tilts his face to the sky as if the sun is shining, but there are thick grey clouds above. He smiles.

20

There is no face behind the glass at the reception, watching him. There is no queue for room sixteen. Jake glides up the stairs and knocks on the door and he holds his breath with anticipation and he waits. He knocks again.

There is movement inside, but she is slow to answer. He half-expected her to remain on the bed and to call, to invite him in from across the room, but he is glad she is coming to the door. He wants to see her face. Wants to see the realisation dawn when she remembers who he is, the bond they created the last time.

She opens the door but doesn't bother to look at him. "Come in," she says, already turning and walking away, crossing the room back to the bed.

He fumbles, then steps quickly after her, closes the door, says "Joanie."

She turns, an eyebrow raised. She looks him up and down, studies his face. He does see the realisation dawn on her, but the surprise and happiness he expected does not come. Her face is blank. "What're you doin here, kid?"

He can't help but feel she calls him 'kid' because she can't remember his name. "It's me," he says. "Jake."

"I remember you. Where's Carl?"

"Carlson?"

"Whatever. Where is he?"

"I don't know. What's it matter?"

"Why're you here?"

He stands, stunned, feels as though he doesn't have a suitable explanation, like he's been caught doing something he shouldn't have, then he remembers and reaches into his pocket and pulls out the bills. "I have money," he says.

Joanie looks at the cash for a long time, then she looks at him. She shrugs her shoulders, holds out her hands. "Kid, I –" She trails off.

Jake frowns, but he keeps his arm outstretched, offering the money.

"I thought I told you – I thought you understood –"

He looks at the money. "It's not enough?"

She looks like she is chewing on something, like she is biting her tongue or the inside of her cheek. She takes the money from him, doesn't count it. "It's enough," she says.

She goes to the bedside drawer, pulls out a condom and passes it to him, then climbs onto the bed. "Put that on," she says.

21

Jake stays awake, waits for Carlson to return. The television keeps him company. It plays black and white films that look old but are unfamiliar and seem foreign, though no one speaks and everyone communicates via hand gestures.

He eats a sandwich. He has survived on sandwiches filled with cold meats and condiments since he came to stay with Carlson. There is no other food. He has never seen Carlson eat and has surmised that he probably does so while he is at the diner.

It is a long time after midnight when Carlson finally returns. Jake sits in darkness but the television is still on and Carlson seems surprised by it.

"Hey," he says.

Jake nods.

"You're still up."

"Yeah."

"Haven't seen you in a while." It has been a few days since they last saw each other. Their paths have rarely crossed. "Wasn't sure you were still stayin here, truth be told." He turns on the light. "Your face is good," he says. "All healed."

"Is that your way of askin me to leave?"

"No, it's just –"

"It doesn't matter. Figure I best be on my way back home soon."

Carlson nods. "Yeah, yeah, exactly. Harry will be worried about you. When was the last time you spoke to him?"

Jake snorts. "He doesn't worry about nothin."

"You're his boy."

"And that's all I am. But that ain't what I wanna talk to you about."

"You wanna talk about somethin?"

"Your diner, Good Eats – there any jobs goin?"

"Like, weekend jobs?"

"Weekend, nighttime – anythin, I don't give a shit. Doin drinks, bussin tables – hell, I'll even try my hand at fryin, I just need to get some money."

"Why's that?"

"Cos I ain't got any."

"What's the rush now?"

"There's no rush. But we all gotta start somewhere."

Carlson opens his mouth and Jake thinks he knows what he's going to say, that he's going to mention Joanie, so he cuts him off.

"I need a job, man. I gotta get some cash together. A day's gonna come I can't live with Harry anymore. I can't stay there forever, you know that. I'm gonna have to get a place of my own. Might as well have a little something to fall back on when that day comes."

Carlson looks thoughtful. "What about school?"

"It's summer vacation. And when I go back I'll just do weekend work, like I said. I'll work around school."

Carlson goes into the kitchen, to the fridge, gets himself a beer. He pops the tab and takes a long drink then says "Just part-time, right?"

"Right."

"Just weekends, you've still got school during the week."

"Maybe a little more round the holidays."

Carlson nods. "Okay." He takes another drink. "Okay. I'll talk to the boss man."

22

Harry looks up from the television as Jake enters the trailer. "Well shit," he says. "Look who's come home. Where the hell've you been, boy?"

"Out," Jake says.

"Jesus Christ boy, you been gone for Lord knows how long now, and you ain't even gonna tell me where you been?"

"With friends," he says. "Where d'you think I've been?"

Harry laughs. "We were startin to get worried, weren't we?" He's talking to Maggie. She is in the kitchen, cleaning plates. She comes into the front room drying her hands on a dish cloth.

"I was," she says.

Harry laughs. "I told her you'd be all right. Told her you can take care of yourself. Said you'd just be stayin with either one of those boys – what they called? Gary and Dave?"

"Ray and Glenn."

"Yeah. Them."

Harry is smoking. The air in the trailer is thick with the cloying smoke of burning marijuana, Jake felt a contact buzz as soon as he stepped into the room. The ashtray on the table in front of Harry is filled with crushed butts and flicked ash. He holds a joint in his hand, he takes a draw from it. His eyes are half-closed and the parts showing from under the lids are red. It looks like he's been smoking since Jake left. He sits in his underwear, light blue boxer shorts and a well-worn vest that started life white but is now rinsed out and grey with patches of brown.

"You were gone an awful long time," Maggie says.

"Said he was with friends," Harry says.

"I heard." Maggie wears a red t-shirt and a pair of denim shorts. Her feet are bare. "Leave that door open some," she says. "Before your daddy smokes us all out."

Jake opens the door a little wider, steps away from it, lets clean air in.

"She wanted to call the police," Harry said. "I had to talk her out of it. See, I knew you'd be okay. You're my boy, you can handle yourself."

"You been worried too," Maggie says.

Harry snorts.

"No good makin that noise. I know you've been lyin awake at night, creepin out here to look out the windows every time you think you hear someone comin close."

Harry grins and waves her off. He turns to Jake. "So why have you come back, today of all days? Somethin special goin on?"

Jake shrugs. "Had to come back eventually."

Harry nods. "That is true. Why don't you go on and get changed, those clothes are lookin a little worse for wear."

"Sure."

"You plannin on leavin us again anytime soon?"

"No. I got a job, though. I wanted to tell you that."

"A job?"

Maggie leans one hip against the counter, folds her arms and crosses one leg over the other. "What about school?"

"It's a weekend job," he says. "A couple of nights, too."

"Doin what?" Harry says.

"At a diner in town. Good Eats – you heard of it?"

Harry scratches the stubble around his mouth, tugs at a corner of his moustache. "Name sounds familiar. What they got you doin there?"

"Little bit of everythin – bussin tables, scrubbin pots. Say they're gonna get me on the fryers, too."

"Don't let it take up too much of your time," Maggie says. "Don't let it get in the way of your schoolwork."

"Hell, Maggie – boy's gotten himself a job!" Harry says. He sounds pleased. "Gonna make himself some money! I'm proud of you, boy."

Jake forces a smile, nods.

"When do you start?"

"Tomorrow."

"Shit, they don't waste no time, do they?"

"Guess not. I'm gonna go get changed."

Harry beams. "Good to have you home, Jacob. When you're ready, come back out here and sit with me a spell. Plenty of this to go round, we oughta celebrate."

Jake goes to his room. Maggie follows him in, closes the door after them. She looks concerned. "You all right?" she says.

They are cramped in Jake's small room. He sits on the bed so they are not stood so close to each other, their breath in each other's face. "I'm fine," he says. "How are you?"

She ignores him. "You been gone a long time."

He shrugs. "Ain't been up to much."

She looks at him sideways, her eyes narrowed. "Somethin's different," she says.

"What?"

"I don't know. You just seem different."

It occurs to Jake that if he were to stand up again they would be close enough to kiss. He could kiss her. She would probably let him. She seems to like him. He thinks about his father in the next room and stays sitting. "Same old me," he says.

"Mm. I'm gonna make some food soon. You gonna sit with us?"

"Yeah."

She nods, then leaves him.

Jake changes his clothes, lies on his bed for a few minutes just to get used to being back home, then goes out to join Maggie and his father.

Harry lights up when he sees him. "Carlson!" he says. Jake freezes. "I knew I knew the name, Good Eats – Carlson works there! Think he's a cook or somethin. When you see him, tell him I say hey, and that he oughtta get his ass back round here sometime."

"Okay." Jake sits down, takes the joint his father offers.

"You remember Carlson? He's been round here a few times before, but it was a long time ago now. We usedta work together."

Behind them, Maggie sets to work in the kitchen, pulling out pots and pans from the cupboard. Jake watches her out the corner of his eye. Her back is to him. She turns enough he can see the side of her face while she works.

"Sure," Jake says. "I think I'll recognise him."

23

Jake walks along the dark streets, his legs tired and his back sore. He can smell grease, the stink of it sunken already into his hair and his skin, permanently up his nose. He passes a drunk taking shelter in a doorway, sucking on a bottle of wine. The drunk raises his hand in greeting, smiles a toothless smile, and Jake nods back.

He's been paid. His first pay cheque. He is going to the motel.

He takes his time up the stairs, his body aching from fifteen hour days spent standing with only short cigarette breaks for respite. After the first shift Carlson took him aside. "If you don't like it, you don't have to keep doin it," he said. "You can find somethin else."

"I never said that," Jake said.

After the second shift, Carlson took him aside. "If you don't like it, just remember you can leave any time. This ain't the end of the road for you."

"I never said that."

After the third shift, Carlson took him aside. "How you doin, you copin? It's tough, I know. It ain't for everyone. If you don't feel cut out for it, just tell me, understand? There's always somethin else."

"I never said that."

After the fourth shift, Carlson clocked out, said goodnight, and was on his way.

Jake reaches room sixteen, knocks. There is no answer. He puts his ear close to the door, can hear noise inside. Occupied. He steps away, leans against the railing, has to wait his turn. He lights a cigarette. There is no queue.

He hasn't finished smoking when the man leaves. They don't look at each other, but Jake studies the other man out the corner of his eye. He is short and fat and most of his hair is gone. Jake waits until he is halfway down the stairs before he knocks.

"Come in."

Joanie is in the bathroom. She stands at the window, smokes, hasn't bothered to dress. "What's that smell?" she says.

"I got a job."

She turns, eyes narrowed, sees him. She looks at him for a long time, looks him up and down. "Uh," she says. "What do you do?"

"I'm a cook."

"Good for you. You smell like burgers."

"That's what I cook, mostly."

"You any good?"

"You just gotta fry them up."

"You're really sellin your business."

"It is what it is."

She snorts. "Ain't it just."

"And it ain't mine."

She nods. "Let me see the money."

Jake shows her the notes.

"Put it on the side."

He does as she says.

She falls silent and finishes her cigarette. Jake stands by the door, watches her. Inside the room, he can't smell himself. All he can smell is the man that was here before him, his sweat still drying on the crumpled bed sheets.

"Take off your clothes," Joanie says. "Get in the bed. I'll be right through."

Jake undresses, presses his clothes to his nose. They stink. He can smell the potato of the fries in there more than anything else, even the burgers. It feels good to take them off. He climbs onto the bed, slides under the blanket, doesn't think about whoever has been here before him, however many of them, doesn't think about the side of the man's face leaving the room before he entered.

He hears Joanie close the bathroom window, hears her bare feet padding across the floor. She puts her cigarette pack down next to the money, then picks up the notes and counts them out. Satisfied, she puts the money away then gets into the bed with him. She doesn't lie down, she stays on her knees. She reaches under the cover, checks him with her hand. He is semi-erect. She gets him the rest of the way.

"How've you been –" Jake starts.

"We don't need to talk," she says.

When he is ready she climbs on top. She doesn't give him a condom. She straightens up and rides him hard and fast. Her face is turned to the side. She looks disinterested.

Jake lies back and closes his eyes, and pretends that she's having a good time.

About the Author

Paul Heatley's short stories have appeared online and in print for a variety of publications. His credits include Thuglit, Horror Sleaze Trash, The Pink Factory, Spelk, Shotgun Honey, and the Flash Fiction Offensive, amongst others. He is also the author of An Eye For An Eye, published by Near To The Knuckle, and the forthcoming Fatboy, due May 2017 from All Due Respect. He lives in the north-east of England.

Printed in Poland
by Amazon Fulfillment
Poland Sp. z o.o., Wrocław